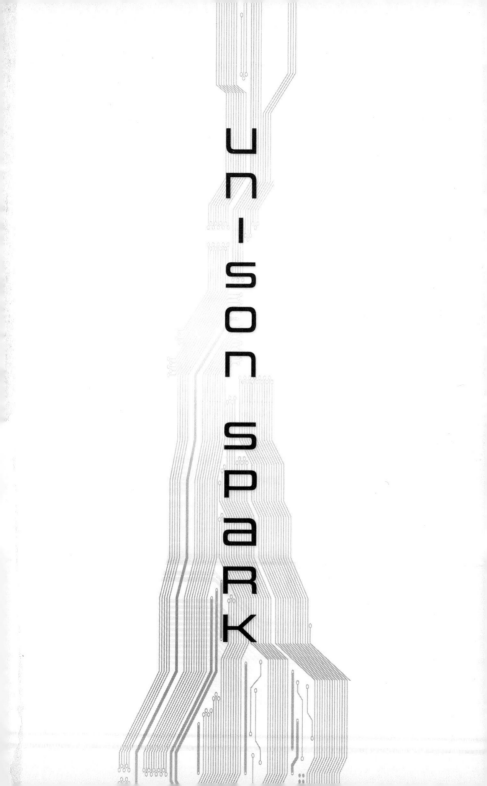

UNISON SPARK

andy marino

unison
spark

henry holt and company

new york

Henry Holt and Company, LLC
Publishers since 1866
175 Fifth Avenue
New York, New York 10010
macteenbooks.com

Library of Congress Cataloging-in-Publication Data
Marino, Andy.
Unison spark / Andy Marino.—1st ed.
p.   cm.
Summary: Fifteen-year-old Mistletoe lives in the subcanopy zone amid poverty
and outdated technology, but when she meets Ambrose Truax, the privileged
sixteen-year-old heir to the Unison empire and they discover they share a sinister link,
they begin a frightening journey into the uncharted territory of the Unison 3.0 upgrade.
ISBN 978-0-8050-9293-6 (hc)
[1. Science fiction.]   I. Title.   PZ7.M33877Un 2011   [Fic]—dc22   2011002864

First Edition—2011 / Designed by April Ward

Printed in October 2011 in the United States of America by R. R. Donnelley & Sons
Company, Harrisonburg, Virginia

10 9 8 7 6 5 4 3 2 1

FOR Lauren

1

THE GIRL WITH
THE bLUE PIGTAIL

HER NEW NAME was Mistletoe. On her fifteenth birthday, she announced to her caretaker, Jiri, that she was sick of being called Anna.

He grunted. "Anna's your name."

"Who picked it out?"

"Your mother and father."

"And where are they?"

He raised a bushy eyebrow. "Okay. What do you want to be—"

"Mistletoe."

She read his face: *that's crazy.* So she added, "Here's how it is: I'll be thinking of myself as Mistletoe, so when you call me Anna, I won't answer. Because that's not my name."

She glared as he rolled his eyes in resignation, the signal that she had won. Jiri plunged his thick fingers back into the hopeless jumble of wires that had once been a genuine pre-Unison computer. Mistletoe went out on the balcony. Lying on her back, she gazed up through the airholes in the plasteel canopy that kept Little Saigon from rising into topside Eastern Seaboard

City. She lived with Jiri at the peak of a mountain of makeshift houses that cascaded down thirty stories to the streets below. Their house was wedged so tightly beneath the canopy that Mistletoe imagined she could feel the weight of the city pressing down upon her as she slept.

She rocked her head gently back and forth until her fluffy blue pigtail flattened into a pillow. The airholes were no bigger than Jiri's fist, but if she lay in just the right spot she could watch gleaming cars pass within teeth-clenching millimeters of one another. The hum of a billion commuters herded by Eastern Seaboard City's traffic control system resonated down through the airholes and rattled her insides pleasantly, like the pre-Unison massage chairs Jiri sold at his junk shop. As the afternoon above the canopy faded to crimson dusk, she drifted into an uneasy dream. . . .

The room was dim and ice-cold. She was strapped to a slab inside a metal tube the size of a refrigerator. Old-fashioned gunshots, raw and booming, punctuated distant shouts. The thudding of disruptor weapons became frantic footsteps. A gentle voice said, "Don't be afraid, Anna."

Cut to a new scene. She was bobbing jerkily up and down. A snake was slithering across her shoulder. No, two snakes. Three! She screamed and found herself muffled, her face buried inside the folds of a man's greasy, foul-smelling overcoat. She squirmed and he clutched her closer to his chest. The snakes were all around her. She tried to bite the meaty hand. The man cursed in a different language. *Jiri!* He was running faster than she'd ever believed possible, squeezing her to his body with one hand while the other fired a pistol backward over his shoulder. She extracted an arm and grabbed hold of one of the snakes.

It was smooth and metallic, some kind of wire. She felt along its length until her hand reached her forehead.

Her face was sprouting wires.

She screamed and wriggled free of Jiri's grasp, and then she was flailing in empty space. She woke before she hit the ground, sitting upright on the balcony, hands pressed against the sides of her wireless head, panting.

Today, six months later, Mistletoe sat on the balcony with her back against Nelson, the rickety scoot she'd rescued from Jiri's junk shop. In the city above the canopy, Nelson was probably some rich kid's discarded toy. Down in her teeming subcanopy neighborhood, he was a treasure worth protecting with her life. The four electrostatic ion lifts on the underside were top-of-the-line ESC craftsmanship. Her friend Sliv had replaced the clattering transmission and aligned the steering. She rarely let the scoot out of her sight.

"I had the dream again last night, Nelson."

The scoot sat silently. It didn't have A.I. components and couldn't hear or respond. Conversations between Mistletoe and Nelson were heavily one-sided.

She sighed and looked through the clear plexi door at Jiri hunched over a tattered old instruction manual, squinting and sounding out the words to himself. She had seen other foreigners read Western English like that. But she had never seen anyone take notes like Jiri, like he was recopying the entire thing. His method seemed ridiculous, but she had never asked him about it, just placed it in the category of things they would never discuss. Since the bad dreams had begun six months ago, that category had grown steadily. Secrets seemed to breed more secrets. And there had always been something hurried and on edge about the way Jiri talked to her, as if he would rather she just kept things to herself. So, most of the time, she did. Her latest secret was a present from Sliv, a necklace with a silver charm of three interlocking gears. He'd never given her anything before, and she'd been too surprised to thank him. She kept it hidden beneath her shirt. The tiny gears inhabited the scooped-out hollow where her collarbone met her throat.

She watched Jiri scratch his mustache and turn the page. He was too busy to notice that she had spent all day out on her scoot without checking in. She hugged her knee to her chest and prodded her shin—bruised from squeezing between a stalled transport bus and a spice-import cart. Tender, but not unbearable.

Across the walkway that swung beneath the canopy, a young couple was tending a fire. Mistletoe waved, but they, too, had no time to spare for her and didn't even look her way. She lay on her back, blue pigtail cushioning her head, and stared up through the holes. She wondered how many other kids were doing the same thing. Every time she imagined *other kids*, she imagined them with her exact thoughts and ideas and questions. She glanced down over the edge of the balcony at the endless jostling masses below—Little Saigon was like a ripe grape with mushy insides too big for its skin—and despaired. Because what did it matter what she thought about anything? She was a speck, a tiny particle who would live and die staring up through a hole while the world went about its business as if she had never been born.

As she often did when she needed a new train of thought,

she pictured Aunt Dita, the only person who ever took her to do anything fun. It was Aunt Dita who helped her pick out just the right scent for her pigtail, jasmine and rye, and helped her dye it blue with mashed-up roots. And it was Aunt Dita who snuck her topside into UniCorp Park's Designated Young Person Recreational Zone, where there were scoot-ramps and a free Unison simulation that was supposedly just like the real thing.

Unison: the grand culmination of all human social networks. BetterLife. The Mass Hallucination. However it was marketed and advertised, it barely mattered to Mistletoe. She couldn't afford the hardcoded ID that allowed access to topside Eastern Seaboard City, much less a coveted Unison login.

Angry curses exploded from inside the house. She turned her head. Jiri slapped an ancient cell phone twice with his huge hand, then threw it hard against the floor. Like all subcanopy residents, he had to try several battered old cells to pick up the faintest of signals, and she always watched the scene—big frustrated man, tiny helpless phone—with puzzled amusement. He picked up another one, pressed a button, and started yelling.

"Yes, but—yes. Is what I said. Of course I am at home, it is where . . ." His shoulders slumped as he lowered his voice. "Now? Yes. Okay. I understand. *Ma buh.*"

He looked out through the plexi, ashen-faced, and did not seem to see her. She waved. Something was wrong. She opened the door.

"Jiri?"

His eyes snapped down to hers. "Come inside. Shut the door. Stay here."

"What's wrong?"

"Stay inside, Anna." He looked so distraught she didn't bother to correct him, just watched as he squirmed into his overcoat and patted the pre-Unison handgun in the pocket. He thought she didn't know about it, but he was always absently tapping it through the fabric. "I come back later."

"Where are you going?"

"Later, I explain." At the door he turned to her again, opened his mouth, hesitated. "If I . . ."

"What?"

"Mistletoe. I forget, always. Stay inside. I see you again later."

The door slammed behind him, and she listened to the hum of the elevator fading down the shaft. She ran to the balcony and located the shiny dot of his bald head among the crowd. He was on foot. Not going far, then. She watched as he elbowed through a trio of yellow- and orange-painted gypsies, knocking one of the men into the ragged procession of buggies and scoots that inched its way through the streets all day and all night. Most people disabled their traffic alarms down here, but some proved frustratingly hard to silence, and Little Saigon was always thick with gentle reminders in a thousand languages to *drive slowly and carefully*, as if there were ever an opportunity to speed on the choked roads. She glanced at Nelson, then turned back to the scene below in time to catch Jiri disappearing behind a shanty-stack down the block, near the cluttered access road where reprogrammed A.I. transports trucked scrap for junk lords. A few more seconds, and she would lose him for good.

She pulled her orange goggles up from around her neck and suctioned them to her eyes. "No way we're staying here, Nelson."

Her scoot was cold, but she cranked it up and hopped on, slipped her hands through the handle straps, and kicked open a trapdoor in the balcony. She had warmed up Nelson on the way down before—ill-advised, maybe, but not impossible. She felt the soft cushion of energy beneath her as the ion lifts whirred to life. The engine sputtered but hadn't yet caught when she tipped the nose through the trapdoor. The lifts barely kept her off her neighbors' roofs as she half drove, half plummeted down the sloped stack of huts. A woman hanging laundry ducked as the nose of the scoot tore several white shirts from the line, scattering them down the stack.

"Watch it!" Mistletoe screamed over her shoulder. Then the lifts fully engaged and she felt the cushion expand beneath her. Near the base of the stack, she nosed up over the crowded street and gave the side of the scoot a swift, hard kick. Static pulled up strands of hair as she sailed over people's heads. Then the engine turned over and she descended between two staggering drunks with green absynthium stains on their shirts. She skidded hard, ducked beneath their outstretched arms, and bounced around the corner, ignoring their cries to come back. As she cruised alongside the access road, she was suddenly aware that her timeworn engine sounded like thunder next to the eerie silence of the junk transports. The older models still made noise, but the lack of cursing and yelling and laughter gave the entire street—the perimeter of Little Saigon—a solemn desolation that freaked her out. And Jiri was nowhere.

Thank you for your business! said one of the transports.

Keep your eye on the ball, children! said another.

Mistletoe shuddered. Cautiously she eased forward. The transports had been rescued from junk heaps, only to have their A.I. circuitry refitted with mindless programs dooming them to a lifetime of carting endless piles of subcanopy garbage. Where did it all go?

Up ahead she heard sudden bursts of gruff speech: Jiri and someone else.

"Whoa, Nelson," she whispered, and eased up on the throttle even more. The scoot purred. She followed the sound of the voices into a narrow, badly paved ditch that ran between the main street and the junk-transport road. A forgotten path, littered with bottles and ragged gray lumps she didn't want to look at very closely. She cut the engine but kept the lifts engaged, and peeked around a pile of rusting scrap. There, in the middle of the road, was Jiri, standing with his back to her, pointing his black pre-Unison handgun at a stocky ESC police officer with a gleaming metallic arm that narrowed to a glowing tip, which was in turn pointed at a boy of about her age who was dressed better than anyone she'd ever seen. His outfit was holo-fashion, an elegant projection of a sharp new suit in the manner of big-time businessmen from up above. His wispy blond hair sparkled, even in the subcanopy shade. He was clearly a long way from home, and his hands were in the air. He shifted his wide eyes from Jiri to the cop.

"I take him," Jiri said.

"Like hell you do," the cop said casually as the tip of his metallic arm flared orange. And to the boy: "You're going home now, kid."

The boy didn't flinch or say a word. Mistletoe idled her scoot. She felt light-headed. The bravado of men like Jiri and the cop made her nervous. Every day she tore through the streets of Little Saigon and witnessed all kinds of human ugliness. And her dream had told her that Jiri and his friends were killers. Or kidnappers. Or both. Deep inside, she believed it. She had a brief, jarring memory of wind howling in her ears, of being clutched to Jiri's chest as he ran. Shooting, screaming, dying. And for what? She thought that maybe even the men themselves didn't know. Maybe they did it for the act itself, for the sickening head rush, the ear-popping high before the crash.

Suddenly she saw a second cop's head rise slowly over the top of the scrap heap, saw this cop raise her own metallic arm—*disruptor*, Mistletoe remembered—and aim at Jiri. With blank determination, Mistletoe kick-started the scoot over the top of the rusty pile. She heard herself yell something incomprehensible, a choked-back scream. The side of the scoot grazed the second cop's head as she ducked, surprised, and fell. Jiri didn't flinch, but the first cop blinked and turned toward the scrap heap. Jiri managed to squeeze off a quick *pop-pop-pop* before the cop's arm flashed bright orange and Jiri's skull and spine appeared briefly through transparent, cell-scrambled flesh. A second later he looked normal again. He swayed slightly and watched as the cop collapsed. Then he turned and caught Mistletoe's shocked gaze as he sank to his knees.

Mistletoe felt bile rise in her throat. What had that disruptor done to Jiri? She watched in a stupor as he opened his mouth and raised his eyebrows pleadingly. Then the life went out of his eyes and he fell forward onto his face.

Her mind was blank but for one thought, distant and spare and clean: *Aunt Dita is my protection now.*

A series of meek coughs snapped her out of her daze. The well-dressed boy was kneeling among the three fallen adults. She pulled up beside him.

"Can you walk?"

He kept his eyes on the ground and managed a shrug.

"We can't stay here," she said. Jiri's ancient weapon had been deafening. People would be along to investigate. Other cops, coming to find their fellow officers down. Not something she wanted to stick around and answer for.

"Get on," Mistletoe said. This time the boy looked at Nelson, then at her for the first time. He opened his mouth, but nothing came out. She read his face: *that thing?* The scoot was tiny, rusted, a hundred years old. Rich Boy probably never traveled in anything less fancy than one of those sleek articulated frame cars she watched through the holes in the canopy.

"*Get on.*" She grabbed for his shirtsleeve. Her hand passed through the projection of navy blue fabric and brushed the tight breathable material of his skinsuit. Ten feet away, the second cop began to stir. The boy swallowed once—she watched the lump in his throat move up and down—and jumped on the back of the scoot. Their combined weight strained the lifts, and Nelson protested with an angry *whirrrr.* The boy put his hands cautiously around Mistletoe's stomach and sneezed as her thick, scented pigtail tickled his nose.

They cruised past a steady stream of oblivious transports. Mistletoe envied their brainless detachment—would it be so bad? Did they remember things from their former lives as A.I. units? Suddenly she felt sick and stopped the scoot. In the final seconds of his life, Jiri had looked at her, and his eyes were full of pain. She retched. The cop's weapon had done something horrible to his insides. She rested her hand on the side of the access wall and threw up again.

"Are you okay?" the boy asked.

She answered with a choked sniffle, wiped her mouth, and kicked the scoot into gear. It lurched forward up a ramp to the street level, where a group of ragged little kids were throwing glitchy holo-dice against an empty crate. All at once, the familiar chaotic sounds and smells of Little Saigon blended with the noise of Nelson's engine. She sped through the middle of the dice players and maneuvered expertly through the crowd, crossed the street, and dismounted at the base of a shanty-stack a few blocks from her own. She was conscious of how close they were to the scene of Jiri's death, and her street instincts told her to go up, always up. She was also conscious of the fact that, behind her, the boy was trying so hard not to cry that his body was twitching in surprisingly violent jolts. She didn't want to look, or she would burst into tears. Her nerves felt raw and exposed.

"Sorry," he mumbled.

"I'm supposed to go to my aunt Dita's if anything happens to Jiri," she said, as matter-of-factly as she could manage. "They made me promise."

The boy twitched once more and was quiet. She led him to the open door of the boxy lift and shoved her scoot inside.

"I'm sorry," he said. "I don't know what else to say. I'm— thank you."

There was a single dark grease smudge on the boy's pale face. Other than that, he looked like he'd just stepped out of a fashion wiki.

"So who are you?" she asked. But before he could speak, her eyes blurred, and hot tears came. The door closed and they ascended.

"I'm—," he began, then stopped and stared at the metal

wall of the lift, where someone had spray painted a wilted orange flower. "This morning I was somebody else."

She blinked away tears, steadied her voice. "You're from topside."

He nodded.

"So what are you doing in Little Saigon?"

He put his palms against the wall of the lift and let himself fall forward until his forehead rested against the center of the flower. Orange petals drooped around his shiny hair. He took a deep breath and let it out.

"It's been a very strange day."

2

THE bOY IN THE bUSINESS SUIT

HIS NAME WAS Ambrose Truax, and his strange day had started just after dawn with a crisp knock upon his bedroom door and a voice that called to him.

"Sir? It's time."

Ambrose swam up out of sleep, away from the dream he'd been having almost every night since he turned fifteen, six months ago. This morning he was left with a slideshow of impressions: cold metal, darkness, his father's voice. He shuddered and blinked away the crust from the corners of his eyes for the last time. After today's modification procedure, he'd never sleep again.

The bedroom, aware of his waking, gradually brightened the window to bathe the room in gentle, lemony sunlight.

Another knock. "Sir?"

Ambrose sat up as his standard morning Process Flow clicked into place in his mind, altered here and there to account for the importance of the day ahead. There would be extra preparations. He yelled toward the door, "Meet you in the hall in seven minutes." Shuffling footsteps receded.

At fifteen, Ambrose was the youngest UniCorp Associate. The next-youngest, a Data Mapping prodigy from the Greater London Expansion, was twenty-one. Ambrose even headed his own Process Flow team, which meant he was responsible for following Friendship threads and predicting user behavior within the Unison social network. This ensured that each Unison login was a singularly satisfying, pleasant, and efficient experience. More than half the world's population paid handsomely for their Unison Profiles, and it was Ambrose's job to make them want to stay logged in forever.

The fact that Ambrose was the son of UniCorp CEO Martin Truax (and richer than Mistletoe could ever imagine) had never been much of an issue for the older Associates for one reason: he was freakishly good at his job. Corporate wisdom stated that the truly gifted Process Flow Associates had a kind of sixth sense for following multiple Friendship threads and Thought-streams to probable outcomes. For Ambrose, this job was simply an extension of the way his mind always worked. He had known it would take exactly seven minutes to get ready for his day before he had a single conscious thought about what he was going to do first, second, or third. In fact, he'd learned long ago that he could alter his routine at any point—stare out the window, drink a second glass of synthesized grapefruit juice— and it would still take exactly seven minutes.

As if to prove this point, he leapt out of bed and went straight to the window. He lived with his older brother, Len, on the 298th floor of the Great Plains Apartments, so named because the neighboring atmoscrapers were almost entirely pasture buildings. From his window a mile above the canopy of Eastern

Seaboard City, Ambrose watched the sun rise over the fields. The morning had dawned blazing hot, and orange sunlight splayed urgently across the neat green rooftops. He pressed his palm lightly against the window to darken the shade against the glare and watched a group of cows—tiny black-and-white-spotted blobs at this distance—graze in one of the fields. They reminded him of the dairy farm on the border of the New England Expansion his family had toured years ago. His father had let Ambrose and Len run free on their own for an hour or two, and together they had annoyed the lab-grown cows all the way to the edge of the pasture. It was surrounded by some kind of near-invisible plexi shield so cows couldn't fall off and crash through the canopy at atmospheric reentry speed, but Len had managed to find a tiny hole.

Ambrose! Here. Len handed him a marble and grinned wolfishly.

What?

Drop it down.

Off the edge?

Yeah, unless you're . . . Oh my God, you're scared. You're such a podcast.

I'm not! I'll do it, just—right here?

Ambrose glanced back across the field. His father was standing with the Gen-Farm manager, chatting and pointing toward the central irrigation chamber, a gleaming cylinder that skewered the building all the way to the top. They were occupied and too far away to see anything specific. He hesitated a few more seconds, then reached back and launched the marble through the hole, palm thwacking hard against the plexi. The marble sailed out into empty space, spun, hung frozen for a millisecond, and disappeared before they could begin to trace its fall. The plexi prevented them from leaning out too far.

Len grabbed his brother's shoulder, looking very serious.

What did you do?

Stoppit, Len.

What if you—

Shut up!

We're so high, it'll catch on fire and make somebody's head explode—maybe a whole entire family, just . . . Len laid his hands on the side of his head and thrust them outward. *Ppgggggkkkkkkk!*

Ambrose bit his lip and glanced out over the edge. They were barely above the hundredth floor. Surely not high enough to—

Len chuckled. *Let's go back.*

But—

You did a good job today, soldier. I'll report you to high command myself and recommend you for the medal of bravery and a promotion out of podcast squad.

Len turned and took off across the dewy field. Ambrose yelled *Hey!* and tried to catch up, but Len, as always, remained a few steps ahead.

At his bedroom window, Ambrose found that he was pressing his forehead against the glass. It didn't matter if an event from his brief childhood had been fun or scary; part of him always wanted to experience it again and again, stacked up against his growing adult responsibilities like old-fashioned casino chips. There was a reason his few friends were all in their twenties: no one else his age could relate to a life of high-pressure corporate decision making.

His dreams were another matter: feverish odysseys that left him panting and spent. He couldn't ditch them fast enough. And they were getting worse: vivid, detailed, recurring nightly in the weeks leading up to today's procedure. His father claimed it was the sleep center in his brain anticipating its death, going all out before it was flicked like a switch into nonexistence.

He placed a palm gently against his synth-table, a sleek silver tray jutting out from the wall next to the window.

He said, "Cinnamon toast."

One second later, the top of the tray opened silently to reveal a piece of perfectly buttered BetterToast, with cinnamon sprinkled evenly along the top. He grabbed it and munched greedily as he palmed open his walk-in closet. UniCorp Better-Food (A Little Taste of Unison in the Real World!) provided a delicious simulation, infused with proper nutrients and a sensory-blinder tag to fool the stomach into feeling full. Because of the infusion, BetterFood was much healthier than the real thing and never spoiled or tasted any different than you'd expect.

Ambrose scarfed his toast in a few quick bites and brushed the crumbs off his chest. The particle sublimator in his bedroom's filtration unit vaporized them before they hit the floor. He thought of his marble falling off the edge of the dairy farm and wondered if the Eastern Seaboard City Council (to which his father belonged) would ever install large-scale sublimators to zap falling debris before it crashed through the canopy and killed a few dozen people down in Little Saigon or Rio II. An instant Process Flow told him it wasn't worth the money, but still . . .

He stepped into the closet, which contained a single black temperfoam skinsuit draped over a hanger. He tapped the suit with his palm to externalize the vast array of clothing options and instantly the room was filled with designer holo-fashion. He walked back and forth between the rows of floating, translucent ghost-pants and ghost-shirts, settling finally on a vintage, twenty-first-century navy blue suit and tie. He vapored the unselected clothes away with a flick of his wrist and pulled on the skinsuit, which clung gently to his body and looked, outwardly, just like the navy blue suit.

He turned to the doorway of his closet and said, "Reflection."

The doorway became dully opaque, then glassy. He leaned in close and smoothed his wispy blond hair. It was the biggest day of his life, and he wanted to look less like a teenager and more like the businessman his father had raised him to be.

He dismissed the mirror and stepped back into his bedroom, where he popped a UniCorp BetterMint and took a last look around. This was the first morning in several years that he had not shimmered into the company's Unison Workspace to begin his day. He felt a deep, anxious twinge in his belly at the thought of what he was missing and pressed his palms together. The hardcoded receptors closed the login circuit and sent a familiar tingle down to the tips of his fingers. He thought of his password—LenSucks—and felt the symptoms of the shimmer: the battery-acid taste most users chewed BetterMints to cover, the gummy tickle in the back of his throat like he was catching a cold, the brief weightlessness. Then pure joy flowed through him. Emotionally, shimmering was like going from a funeral to a tropical vacation in the blink of an eye.

Ambrose always noticed the enhanced light first, the way it sharpened the edges of his bedroom furniture and brought the room into perfect sparkling focus. It was as if his real life was lived behind a smeared lens and Unison simply wiped it clean. Many users described the experience as truly *seeing* their own surroundings for the first time. Others claimed it was like being a fully aware newborn. His bedroom didn't disappear or change into some impersonal virtual lobby; early Unison quality-assurance tests had determined that shimmering into a drastically different place was disorienting and unpleasant. In theory, users liked the idea of logging in from their home and emerging suddenly into the Swiss Alps. In practice, this induced vomiting, headaches, and the sensation of having water up your nose.

As a high-level Associate, Ambrose could have chosen to shimmer into Admin-only locations like Workspace or Greymatter, his father's estate. But this morning he only had time for a quick update. A mirror appeared in his mind, separating his perception into two distinct sections: the inner world of his Admin Deck and the outer world of Unison. He filtered out all non-UniCorp information—countless Friend requests and Event invitations he never had time to sift through—and accessed the corporate Feed. It felt as if his mind had been opened and arranged for his perusal, and filtering the staggering barrage of information was as simple as closing one door and opening another. His corporate Feed listed Unison activity since he had shimmered out yesterday evening. He absorbed the updates:

43,987 New Accounts
3,499 Accounts sent to purgatory for nonpayment

He accessed the new Accounts and instructed the Deck to rank them according to potential profitability. One of the perks of being Martin Truax's son was that his Process Flow team got first dibs on the richest new users. Today's number one was Lori Frederick-Smith, a plasteel heiress from Boston Heights. She was currently logged in. He turned the mirror outward and displayed her Profile information in his bedroom.

Instantly, he was standing among the swirling details of her life. She was sixty-four, but had upgraded her Account to look young and beautiful. He watched as her tall blond avatar accepted Friendships at a high-society welcome brunch for new users. She moved among them with ease and confidence, shaking hands and air-kissing cheeks. He accessed her Thoughtstream:

Lori Frederick-Smith thinks she wouldn't mind staying here forever.

Ambrose smiled. The world's elderly population had been hesitant to embrace radical new social networking technology, until a recent Eternal Youth in Unison marketing campaign targeted sixty- to hundred-year-olds. New users in this age group now accounted for a huge chunk of UniCorp's yearly revenue. Profits, as his father would say, had been effectively maximized.

Ambrose forwarded Ms. Frederick-Smith's Profile information to his team with instructions to assign her a series of young, wealthy Friends who were almost—but not quite—as attractive as she. Unison had already begun to analyze her likes and dislikes and change itself accordingly; his team would take care of the rest. In a few days, the previous sixty-four years of her life would fade into dismal obscurity as she moved through a world designed solely for her happiness.

He felt a soft nudge against his leg. Lincoln, his UniPet dog, glanced up at him.

"Sorry, boy," Ambrose said, ruffling the brown fur on Lincoln's head. "I gotta go." Lincoln spread his wings and flew up to the ceiling, where he perched upside down like a giant furry bat. Ambrose made a face and wondered why he'd ever thought a flying dog would be cool. Instantly, Lincoln disappeared from the ceiling and reappeared nudging his leg. His wings were gone.

"Good boy," Ambrose said. Then he pressed his palms together and shimmered out. He blinked. His real-world bedroom looked drab and messy. He felt disconnected from humanity, absent from the never-ending stream of vital information. Loneliness gnawed at him. The urge to shimmer back in was almost overwhelming, but he recognized it as a symptom of the logout and took a deep breath.

"Away for ten hours," he told the room. Silently, it calibrated a delicate climactic balance to conserve energy in his absence. In a few seconds he would actually join the physical commute, what his brother Len called the Fleshbound Parade. He took a deep breath and wondered if his life would look different out of ever-sleepless eyes, then turned and palmed open the door.

Time to go to work.

UniCorp headquarters occupied the top twenty-five floors of the UniCorp Building, a 375-story atmoscraper. It was one of the first buildings to be fitted with a red plasteel/brick polymer to make the entire mile-high facade look like a hundred pre-Unison firehouses stacked on top of one another. Around the time of Ambrose's birth, UniCorp had occupied the entire building. Unison Version 2.0 went live soon after, and then every month more empty office space was converted to luxury apartments as thousands of Associates fled office life for the comforts of working entirely within Unison.

For security reasons the UniCorp building had street-level parking only. Mr. Danielson, an elderly Associate who had known the Truax family forever and served as Ambrose's driver and escort, descended smoothly beneath the elevated traffic stream and parked in his designated space. Ambrose glanced up at the bluish-white ion lift patterns traced in the sky by the undersides of tightly packed cars flowing past in perfect harmony. Danielson palmed open the car door for him and smiled. "You ready for the big day, sir?"

Ambrose shrugged. He'd already been through so many preliminary tests and scans over the past year that it was hard to imagine today as an ending point. But it was also hard to deny the fact that today's procedure carried a new kind of weight. All the testing had been performed in Unison. Now they'd actually be invading his physical, fleshbound self and permanently altering the hypothalamus part of his brain, where the sleep impulse lived.

He stepped out into the morning air, warm even in the deep shade of the UniCorp atmoscraper.

"I guess I was born ready," he said in his half-serious businessman voice. Danielson's smile froze for a moment before he slapped Ambrose gently on the shoulder.

"That's the spirit. Reminds me . . . you know, I played football when I was your age—and I don't mean the old American kind. I'm not *that* ancient, despite what your father tells you."

"He says you're old enough to be *his* father."

Danielson extended a hand and flipped it palm side up. His homepage—UniCorp Admin login—sprang from his palm and displayed in the air between them. It was translucent and looked backlit from both sides. Danielson navigated by poking the floating site with his finger and sliding it out of view, the hardcoded browser following his instructions. He landed on a wikisite called *Notable Eastern Seaboard City Births*.

"Okay, Mr. D, I believe you," Ambrose said.

Danielson flipped his palm again and the site vapored away. "These are exciting times, sir."

Ambrose nodded and followed Danielson past carefully tended shrubbery and through the glass doors. His Process Flow abilities, always murmuring on autopilot in the back of his mind, indicated that the procedure would usher in a new phase of his young life, in which Unison would easily surpass plasteel as the most important human invention of all time. His father's careful preparations ensured no other outcome.

The pair's hardcoded security tags opened another set of doors, and they strolled into the crowded lobby, where Ambrose stopped, transfixed. He had not been to UniCorp HQ in years, and things had certainly changed. The cavernous room was a museum for every innovation in social networking, right up to the current Unison Version 2.0, a demonstration of which was projected twenty-five feet above their heads. And the demos were actually functional; he watched a weary teacher usher a group of little kids around twin screens—screens!—displaying Facebook and MySpace, or as Martin Truax called them, the great-grandparents of Unison. The teacher clicked an antique mouse and a series of boxy faces appeared. Ambrose wondered if the creators of those networks had even bothered with Process Flow and shuddered. How did they maximize profits without knowing exactly what people were going to do with their Accounts?

"Funny, isn't it?" Danielson asked.

"What?"

"How people used to accept being anchored to a screen and a keyboard. Seems like it ignores the basic fact about human beings."

"What's that?" Ambrose knew, but played along.

"We're all animals, and animals hate to be trapped."

As they threaded their way across the lobby, Ambrose paused at the U-Space exhibit, the first major transition away from screenbound social networking. It was way before his time, and so primitive looking that he laughed out loud. Glitchy, stuttery avatars—simple projections—viewing hovering text, manually adding Friends to their lists. It was embarrassing, and he felt a strange sort of gratitude at being born in this exact place and time.

U-Space had been short-lived. It was too much like a game and too little like the real world. People wanted something familiar, an enhanced version of reality, where everything ran smoothly. But U-Space did one thing right: it paved the way for a young genius named Martin Truax, who emerged from out of nowhere with his revolutionary BetterLife networking model.

Martin Truax forbade his programmers to simply refactor existing code. Unison would be constructed from the ground up, its pieces designed by small teams of Associates dedicated to the philosophy that Danielson had just repeated for the millionth time: human beings are animals, and animals hate to be trapped. Independent ideas would then be analyzed and integrated into early stages of development or stripped for bits of code and rejected. The result was something radically new that still felt like an old friend the very first time you logged in.

Ambrose wandered in front of Danielson, feeling increasingly dreamy as he moved past the Unison Version 1.0 display. It was a decent imitation of the real world: you logged in and walked around your house, your neighborhood, your school, but everything seemed better—there was no waiting in lines, information flowed freely and easily, Friendships and Activities were predetermined from Process Flows and prescreens. Real-world problems melted away. Widespread contentment became the rule rather than the exception. Ambrose scrutinized the Version 1.0 demonstration until its flaws became apparent: the clunkiness, the glitches and delays as people entered crowded places. He watched as a shopping mall (scaled down to fit inside the roped-off exhibit space) blinked and froze hundreds of people mid-purchase. He shook his head. The hazards of 1.0.

Danielson was somewhere behind him now, hidden in the rush-hour crowd. Straight ahead sat one of several fountains that dotted the lobby floor. One side of the fountain was hidden by a sharply sloping wall, which Ambrose leaned against as he looked up at Version 2.0. This, he knew, was a genuine real-time projection of actual events in Unison. He wondered what it was like to see it here for the first time. He imagined being a normal kid on a field trip, standing in the middle of the lobby and looking up at—

"Mr. Ambrose." A soft voice to his left. He turned. A building security cop in a black UniCorp windbreaker, stunner baton dangling from his belt, disruptor slung across his back. Ambrose smiled.

"I don't have a pen."

People who approached him for an autograph outside of Unison liked to do so the old-fashioned way. They were always much older, and the novelty of a boy genius in their midst made them awkwardly reverent.

The man extended a hand. "Welcome to your building, sir. It's a pleasure to finally meet you." His smile widened into a toothy grin.

When they shook, Ambrose felt the tiny jolt of an unauthorized message transfer, which his own palm receptors should have blocked since he hadn't given permission to accept. The smiling guard had hijacked his email filters.

"*Carpe somnium,*" the guard said, dropping his hand.

"What?" Ambrose tried to place the man's face, voice, handshake. Nothing. "Wait!"

It was too late. The guard melted into the crowd and disappeared. Ambrose tried to follow, but the crush of tourists and fleshbound commuters starting their day had intensified. He found himself boxed in, then pushed back toward the fountain. Danielson was nowhere to be seen. Ambrose rubbed his palm, which throbbed in the aftermath of the hijacking. The message transfer had taken him completely by surprise; probably just the excitement of the day interfering with his Process Flow ability. Any big deviation from the daily routine tended to throw the whole system into chaos.

"Danielson?" he called out. A young girl gazed at him with huge green eyes—color-modded for intensity—until her mother yanked her away. Was this another one of his father's tests? Or one of Len's pranks? He could try to unspool those particular Process Flows and figure out exactly what his family might have planned for him. Or he could just access the message. Why not? It would only take a second.

He looked around for a private corner, but great masses of tourists and Associates surged everywhere. Next to him, a purple-hatted UniCorp Ambassador was leading a group of awestruck children beneath the 2.0 projection. Beyond the group was the café, and beyond that a series of doors that led to the courtyard. He turned practically sideways and edged his way through the crowd, into the bustling café, and out into the vast center courtyard, which was weather-programmed opposite the current season. Outside it was a balmy and cloudless summer day, which meant the courtyard was having a blizzard.

His skin tingled as his suit adjusted to the cold and he paused to look around the mostly deserted space. It had been designed as a showcase for public art and was currently displaying massive plasteel sculptures of Mexican cuisine. He trudged through the ankle-deep snow and ducked behind a hulking enchilada, where he externalized his message transfer log. A simple white inbox floated above his upturned palm. One new message, an audio file with the subject line DREAMS = TRUTH.

He cupped his palm over his right ear and listened. Female voice. Slight Eastern European accent.

"*Carpe somnium,* Ambrose Truax. First thing: I cloaked this file, but you know how UniCorp skims snag traces. So listen carefully because it plays only once. Sorry about the ambush. I wanted to get acquainted long before today, but my colleagues disagreed." She sniffled, paused, and sneezed violently. Ambrose blinked. She continued. "I wish I had more time, but we all wish that. So here's what you must do. Get out of the building right now. Hitch a ride, steal a car, whatever you need to get away. Your waking life is not your own—don't let him take away your dreams, too. He wants to destroy the only piece of you that knows the truth. And then he'll own you completely. Don't let this happen, Ambrose. I can help you. Get to Little Saigon, and go to the—"

Ambrose yanked his palm away from his ear, deleted the transmission, and wiped the transfer log history. *Nice try,* he thought. These so-called terrorists were more pathetic than dangerous. It was like his father always said, when you're on top, everybody wants a piece of you. And if they can't have a piece of you, they want to drag you down to their level. Steal a car? Who did they think he was?

The message actually reinforced the necessity of today's procedure, he told himself. Running UniCorp required constant vigilance. Once he became accustomed to a life without sleep, he'd be able to keep a round-the-clock eye on Unison, working constantly to ensure the continued growth and profitability of the empire that would one day belong to him and his brother.

He hunched over to avoid a swirling mass of snow and wondered idly how the terrorists had managed to plant the fake guard. That was slightly more impressive than the normal anti-Unison disruptions, which mostly consisted of small-time ID hijacks and Account deletions. And how did they know about the procedure?

Well, whatever. There were dozens of ways for classified information to become unclassified within such a massive corporation. He'd figure it out eventually.

But first, his father was expecting him.

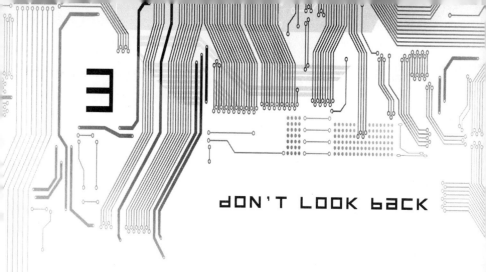

dON'T LOOK bACK

"**HOLd IT**," Mistletoe said.

Until now, she'd let Ambrose tell the story of his day without interrupting, his words echoing around the inside of the lift. They'd stalled at the top of a shanty-stack a few blocks from her own, but the boy hadn't seemed to notice. He was trying to make sense of the past few hours. Mistletoe knew how he felt. One minute she had been daydreaming on the balcony; the next minute she was watching Jiri die.

"The lady in your ear, on the phone or whatever, said *Carpe somnium*? Are you sure?"

Ambrose ran a finger along the stem of the orange graffiti flower. "I'm sure. The security guard said it, too. It means—"

"*Seize the dream*. In Latin. I'm not a friending idiot. Dita and Jiri say it all the time."

She slapped the lone button on the wall. The doors slid open, creaking in protest. Ambrose stared, transfixed. "Everything's so old down here," he said.

She shoved him.

Harder than she'd meant to.

His back slammed the wall and his mouth dropped open as she got between him and the exit. She almost laughed at how shocked he looked—this boy wasn't used to being pushed around. She got in his face.

"Jiri was my friend, okay? And he died saving you." She wasn't exactly sure about either of those things, but it sounded dramatic. "Remember that next time you feel like telling me my neighborhood is old, or smelly, or crowded, or noisy, even though it's all those things, just because you're from topside and . . ." She leaned closer and sniffed him. He shrank back as far as he could. "You smell like a fruit salad."

He swallowed. "It's synthetic citrus essence cologne. From Brussels."

"From *where*?"

"Brussels, a city in—"

"Just, whatever. Shut up. Come on." She eased Nelson out of the lift and waited for Ambrose to hop on the back. He situated himself slowly and gingerly, as if Nelson was some kind of malfunctioning transport that could fling them off at any moment.

"He doesn't bite, you know."

They followed a narrow path that bumped along the top of the shanty-stack next to a dull gray wall lined with windows, the glass long gone and replaced with pockmarked bricks, wooden boards, or nothing at all. The peeling cream-colored underside of the canopy was just above their heads. Hundreds of little houses like the one she'd shared with Jiri were huddled beneath them, sloping down to the street. Roads like lazy rivers divided the stack into haphazard tiers.

"What is this place?" Ambrose asked.

She looked around, puzzled, before reminding herself that he was seeing each part of her neighborhood for the first time. It was impossible to put herself in his shiny black shoes and unknow the familiar places of her daily life. When Aunt Dita had snuck her topside to visit the Designated Young Person Recreational Zone, she'd felt untethered without the canopy overhead, as if she could simply float away from the surface of the earth and never stop going up. Maybe Ambrose was feeling the opposite: trapped.

"You know your big office buildings and apartments?" she asked.

"Atmoscrapers. I live in one."

"Ever been to the bottom?"

"Of course. My favorite restaurant's in the lobby, where they serve this—"

"No, not the *lobby*, twitterbrain. The bottom." Anxious as she was to get to Aunt Dita's, she slowed for Ambrose to take it all in. Once again, she noticed that her scoot's engine was startlingly loud this far from the streets of Little Saigon. She wished she could afford a muffler.

Ambrose ran a hand lightly along the gray wall, leaving a faint finger trail in the grime. "The bottom . . ."

Mistletoe waited for him to blurt out the rest of his delayed understanding, but that was all he said. So she gave him the short history of subcanopy life she'd pieced together from conversations with Jiri and Aunt Dita.

"Plasteel was invented. Buildings started to hit the clouds. Nobody who could afford a place up high wanted to live way down low. So the bottom floors were for people like me and Jiri, but after a while people like you decided it was too dangerous having rich people and poor people in the same building. They evacuated the first thirty stories and filled in the floors with extra plasteel support beams so nobody could move back in. Eventually they were all like that. We built houses up the sides of your buildings; you laid down the canopy. It was all just a big back and forth."

"There were riots," Ambrose said gently, like he was correcting a well-meaning but misguided child.

Mistletoe imagined elbowing him in the face and tossing him down the slope, but instead she clenched the handlebars until her knuckles turned white and kept her eyes on the pathway ahead. She tried to push away the mental image of the blood-spattered cop and Jiri's silent agony, but the scene was burned into her memory. A wave of nausea compressed her throat and stomach. *I'm coming, Aunt Dita,* she thought.

"It wasn't civilized society anymore," Ambrose continued. "It was chaos. The ESC Canopy Division Law was necessary because people were killing each other. It's all archived. Look, I can show you footage of the press conference." He held up his hand next to her face and flipped his palm.

Nothing happened.

She raised an eyebrow as he flipped it again. "What are you doing?"

"I can't get online. No signal."

"You use your *hand* for that?" She kept her eyes forward and hugged the wall as three ancient scoots sped past in the opposite direction, trailing pungent oil-based fumes.

"What do you mean? Everyone—" He paused, then started again. "It's all embedded into the top of my spinal cord. Hard-coded receiver, transmitter, ID tags. I can externalize information through my palm. Up above it's . . . not so strange."

Mistletoe remembered that she had seen people palm-flipping in news footage. Externalizing. Big piles of information springing up out of hands and then disappearing into thin air just as quickly.

"Down here we need cells. And the signal's always weak, if we can get one at all," she explained.

"But it's a free signal," he said. "And it's everywhere."

She shrugged. "Up there, maybe." They passed a row of mangy black dogs curled up next to the wall. The ones who were awake eyed them lazily, pink tongues lolling out the sides of their mouths. She felt Ambrose tighten his grip on her midsection.

"They probably won't bite," she said.

Ambrose swallowed. "So this wall with the broken windows is the side of an apartment building?"

"The thirtieth floor. As high as anybody can pile a house."

They passed an unblocked window, open to the dark interior of the building.

"What's inside, then?" he asked. "Empty floors? How much space is between the support beams? Surely thousands of people can still live there. Has anyone ever renovated?"

"No," Mistletoe said. "No one goes in there." She shuddered.

"Why not?"

"I mean, no one who goes in ever comes out."

"That's ridiculous."

"You wouldn't go in, either, if you knew about it. You wouldn't even go near a window."

The path dipped sharply and dropped them onto a sagging bridge made of boards lashed together with twists of blackened wire. Nelson adjusted to the staccato bumps.

"Knew about what?" Ambrose asked, the words rising shrilly as the houses beneath the bridge gave way to empty space.

"Nothing." She didn't want to talk about the Scourge. Not now, not ever. "We're almost to Aunt Dita's. She'll know what to do."

"Who's she?"

"Jiri's sister."

"No, I mean, what does she do for a living? What's her contribution to society?"

"Contribution to society?"

Ambrose was the strangest boy she'd ever met. She wondered how long he would have survived on the streets of Little Saigon if she hadn't found him. Probably about two minutes. What had Jiri wanted with him?

She gunned the scoot across the bridge and skidded hard onto the path at the peak of a new stack. The lifts protested with a piercing mosquito hum. Ambrose squeezed the air out of her lungs. She elbowed him in the stomach, so he eased up.

Aunt Dita lived a few tiers below the peak. Mistletoe slowed to a crawl and turned off the mostly empty upper path onto a winding street choked with people and dogs. They fell in behind a painfully slow gypsy cart overflowing with vivid shawls and bags labeled COFFEE, which Mistletoe knew probably contained either guns or Little Saigon's latest drug of the month. A rickety transport hauling some kind of antique salvage—power cords and busted screens—pulled up behind them, boxing them in. Mistletoe felt her patience wear perilously thin as they crept along at a slug's pace. She bit the inside of her lip to keep from screaming.

"How many people live in there?" Ambrose asked, pointing to a tiny yellow hut squeezed between two dingy brown hovels. *A lemon sandwich,* thought Mistletoe.

"Probably a whole family," she said. As if on cue, a woman came to the door, bouncing a tiny baby in her arms. A second later a little boy burst from the hut, slid between her legs, and ran off into the crowd. The woman glanced around in bored detachment, sniffed the air, made a face, and stepped back inside.

"Where do they put everything?" Ambrose asked.

"What everything?"

"Their . . . stuff."

"You're the stupidest friending smart person I've ever met," Mistletoe said. "Can't you use that Process Flow thing you were just bragging about to answer your own question?"

"It doesn't work like that. A Process Flow is a *process*—it's based on extensive research and analysis."

"Sounds like it's just guessing."

"It's not *guessing,* and it's not magic. I can't predict the future. I can just apply what I know about people's habits to help the Unison programmers create a series of satisfying outcomes based on a user's spending habits and Friends." The pride in his voice was unmistakable. "I help make people's lives better without them ever having to ask."

"Whatever," she sighed. "They don't *have* anything, Ambrose."

"Who?"

"That lady, her kids. Everybody down here. You don't worry about running out of space in your house when you don't have money to buy things to fill the space."

The gypsy cart rattled away to the left. She sped forward three more blocks, weaving through a line of scoots, and took a sharp right onto a quiet street lined with teardrop-shaped shrubbery. Aunt Dita always said that living down here meant they all had a part to play in making it beautiful. Although she tended the shrubs herself, watering and pruning every day, there were still dry, brown patches. Even the UV-infused canopy lights couldn't make up for the complete lack of sun.

"Nice street," Ambrose said eagerly. Mistletoe recognized overcompensation when she heard it.

Suddenly she cranked Nelson off the road and cut the engine. This time she was glad Ambrose was clinging to her like a crab, otherwise he probably would have been sprawled on the ground. She kept the lifts engaged and hid behind a shrub, nosing forward so that she could peek up the street at Aunt Dita's house.

Ambrose leaned forward. "What are you—"

"Shhhhh!" she hissed. "Something's wrong."

Two men stood on the single step in front of Aunt Dita's bright blue door. Both were tall and thin, with clothes that looked topside: tan suits, not holo like Ambrose's but still too nice for the neighborhood. One man had short red hair and carried a small metal baton. The other man wore a shapeless brown hat and had a silver hand like the cop who'd killed Jiri.

Three other men disappeared down the narrow alley between Dita's house and her next-door neighbor's.

"*Ma buh,*" Mistletoe whispered. "What now?"

"I don't know," Ambrose said. He sounded genuinely shocked to hear himself say that. Mistletoe remembered that his Process Flow was thrown off by unfamiliar situations. Well, what good was it then?

"Use your hardcoded whatever," she said. "Find out who they are."

"How am I supposed to get online? You people are all practically unplugged down here."

Mistletoe let the *you people* slide. "Well, we can't just sit here."

"Call her. Warn her."

"Call her on what? Jiri smashed most of the cells, and I didn't bring one anyway. Not like anybody ever calls me."

"That's ridiculous," he snapped. "How could you not— what are you doing?"

She revved Nelson and shot forward out of her hiding place. She wrenched the scoot into a high-gear burn up the street toward Dita's front step. Ambrose engaged his death grip around her belly and screamed. That was fine. Noise was the whole idea. She joined in with a piercing shriek and bore down on the two men.

Red pulled Hat's shoulder back and pointed at the onrushing scoot. Hat raised his gleaming silver arm and Mistletoe swerved. The frayed burn of an electrostatic pulse missed them by inches. Ambrose buried his face in her pigtail.

Hat got off one more pulse, too high, before Mistletoe was practically up his nose. The two men dove out of the way. As she swerved again to avoid slamming into the half-open door, she thought she caught frantic movement inside the house.

"Hold on!" she yelled, as if Ambrose needed encouragement. Aunt Dita's street dead-ended into the side of an absynthium bar, and they were about to hit it. She threw both heels out straight and slammed Nelson's emergency brake. As the skid took hold, she yanked the handlebar as hard as she could to the left and held it. Ion lifts churned and crackled. Ambrose and Mistletoe leaned parallel to the street. The wall kept coming. Time slowed down enough for her to read a faded poster: DON'T BELIEVE. Don't believe what? Suddenly Ambrose grabbed the handlebar over the top of her hand and pulled. Nelson spun, sputtered, and stopped, tail bumper inches from the wall.

Mistletoe let out a long breath she hadn't realized she'd been holding and looked back down Dita's street.

It was empty now except for the teardrop shrubs, one of which they'd sideswiped. Brittle, papery leaves were settling in their wake. Mesmerized and scared, she watched the last leaf drift to the ground. The wrong kind of charge was in the air—and not just from Hat's arm cannon.

The silence lasted less than a second before the explosion sent Aunt Dita's door spinning across the street, trailing orange flames and black smoke. The noise came right behind the flash, a sharp pop in her ears and a deep thud in her chest. Up and down the street, the tinkle of shattered glass. Nelson rocked back against the wall.

"What was that?" Ambrose squeaked.

But Mistletoe could only watch, numb, as the roof of Aunt Dita's neat little hut collapsed in on itself, on the people inside, on the big pile of blankets Mistletoe curled up in when she was tired, on the shelf full of real dried fruit, on the miniature self-watering greenhouse they'd bought together at the New

Egyptian Market. The greenhouse had only ever produced tiny, malnourished carrots. It had become their favorite joke: we'll never go hungry again!

She saw all these things in an overlapping flash.

Then she snapped out of it and gave Nelson's throttle a nudge forward. "We have to see if she's in there."

"We can't just—"

She pulled up sharply as Hat and Red burst from the thick cloud of smoke engulfing the street in front of Dita's house, riding sleek black ESCPD scoots complete with little round gyrostabilizers for high-speed cornering.

"*Cops*," she hissed.

"Cops don't try to kill you for no reason."

"Maybe not where you're from." She glanced left: more wall. But to the right there was an impossibly narrow alley, half hidden by a crumbling piece of green stucco that drooped off the side of the bar.

Believe, she thought, and drove Nelson straight at the bottom of the entranceway where the stucco hadn't yet fallen. Another crackling pulse singed her pigtail. She hoped Ambrose still had a face and yelled, "Elbows in!"

She hit the entranceway fast and didn't slow down. The sides of Nelson's handlebar scraped the wall, igniting a shower of sparks. If the alley narrowed, they'd stop short and sail forward without the scoot. She nosed up over a pile of greasy clothes that might have been a dead man.

Up ahead the alley widened and emptied onto the street behind Dita's. Almost there! Except now a dark shape blocked the exit. One of the cops, silhouetted against the relative daylight of the street, bobbing up and down on his idling scoot.

How did he get there so fast? She could just barely make out the outline of his—

"Hat!" yelled Ambrose.

Mistletoe slammed her thumb down on a red button marked HL for the first time ever, praying for enough leftover hyperlift fumes from Nelson's former life to power the jump.

There turned out to be plenty.

The scoot roared straight up as the cop fired, his pulse crackling beneath them by several feet. Mistletoe's stomach felt like it was being sucked down into her legs. She gritted her teeth and tried to steer as they cleared the top of the alley and kept rising. Sliv must have tweaked the hyperlifts, too. She wondered if she'd made a huge mistake, then Nelson slowed and seemed to freeze in the air at the very top of the jump. As they hung, suspended, she looked out across the rooftops, jagged and tightly packed like a mouth with too many teeth, and caught sight of the swirling black smoke that had been Aunt Dita's house. Above them the canopy stretched endlessly toward oblivion.

Then they fell.

Ambrose squeezed so hard, Mistletoe feared he'd crush her ribs. She tried to steer toward a flat-topped hut, but the hyper-lift had transferred power from the ion lifts and without them, Nelson was dead weight. She gave the side of the scoot a swift kick like she'd done so often careering down her own shanty-stack. They were going to hit hard.

Another heel-bruising kick.

The lifts engaged. The scoot bounced off the static cushion just before they hit the roof. Instantly, she considered their next move. Her brain was moving in a series of rapid-fire jump cuts, her actions controlled by something other than conscious thought.

Go up, it told her. *Always up.*

Behind her, Ambrose let out a huge breath.

"Bet you wish you lived down here," she said over her shoulder as she jumped to the next roof.

"You do this a lot?"

She shook her head. "First time."

She weaved through the maze of clotheslines, doghouses, and low-grade signal boxes that littered the rooftops of Little Saigon, winding ever upward. A few blocks from the top of the stack, she rode the slope of an A-frame hut down to the street, tucking in behind the gypsy cart they'd seen earlier.

"Not this friending thing again," she said, and darted around a corner.

Ahead of them in the road was Red, idling and scanning the crowd.

Who are *these guys?* she thought. How do they know all the shortcuts?

"Behind!" screamed Ambrose. She turned to look as Hat popped out from around the corner. He'd been right on their tail.

"Keep going up," Ambrose urged. He was right: she'd rather take her chances with Red than with Hat and his arm cannon, even if his aim was a little poor. They'd been lucky so far.

She gunned Nelson up the middle of the street. Pedestrians dove to the side. Red turned to face them and held his metal baton out straight. Mistletoe yanked Nelson to the left, knocking a kid off his pedal bike. The baton seemed to extend in a series of quick flashes, and an unlucky woman in the place they'd just been fell instantly to her knees, hands behind her back, head bowed in peaceful submission. Mistletoe sideswiped an absynthium cart and the neon green liquid splashed Red in the face. He dropped the baton—a police-issue stunner—and slapped his palms over his eyes, wobbling on the scoot.

That's gonna burn like hell, she thought with a surge of glee as they zipped past him toward the upper road.

"Other one's still behind us," Ambrose said.

She couldn't have told him how the plan formed in her mind, or why she didn't immediately think of a more reasonable one. But there it was, laid out like something she'd been planning for days.

"He won't follow us where we're going," she announced as they left the edge of the crowd and cruised onto the upper road.

"Where?"

"In here," she said, aiming straight for one of the empty windows set into the wall of the thirtieth floor.

"I thought you said—"

But the silence was so abrupt as they entered the building that Ambrose choked back his words before they could echo. Darkness engulfed them. She eased up on the throttle and spun around, waiting, panting. The bustling world on the other side of the window seemed remote and hazy, as if they'd passed through several distinct airlocks. After a few seconds, Hat's silhouette appeared in the window and bobbed as he idled his scoot. She held her breath and shrank back into the darkness. Ambrose tightened his grip on her aching ribs. Hat bobbed there for so long she wanted to scream, and then he disappeared.

She crept farther inside, aware that even the quietest scoot would sound like an earthquake in here. Nelson didn't exactly purr, but she couldn't abandon him.

Far below, something rumbled. The building seemed to shiver, its plasteel guts rattling like bones.

The Scourge.

She cut the engine. The noise stopped. Too afraid to turn on the headlight, she pried herself out of Ambrose's grip and hopped gingerly down onto the hard floor. She felt around until she came to a wall, or one of the huge plasteel beams.

"Over here," she whispered. Ambrose joined her. A few feet away, Nelson sensed the absence of riders and quietly went to sleep.

Mistletoe's mind reeled as the jump cuts began to unspool. Jiri. Ambrose. Dita. The cops. And what now? What came next? They couldn't sit here in the dark forever.

Aunt Dita. She didn't want to think about it. She reached out and grabbed Ambrose's softly manicured hand, instantly conscious of her own calluses and cuts. Together they slid down the wall and sat close in the silence. She listened to the pounding of their hearts slow gradually, beat by beat. This boy was strange and annoying, but she had to admit that it felt nice to be pressed against his warm body after such a frantic escape.

"Tell me the rest," she whispered, finally.

"The rest . . ."

"You ignored the message from the lady. *Carpe somnium, Ambrose Truax.* You went up to see your father."

"I don't think it really . . . I mean, right now?"

"I just need to hear it, okay? I need to hear something or I'll go crazy."

Jiri's pleading eyes. Aunt Dita's exploding house.

"Okay," he said. "I ignored the message. It seemed crazy, and it was time to get on with it—my father was waiting on the top floor."

Mistletoe closed her eyes.

The darkness was the same.

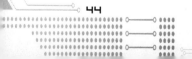

4

AMBROSE TRUDGED BACK across the snowy court-yard of UniCorp HQ, retracing the fuzzy edges of his filled-in shoe prints. Inside the lobby he glanced around for the guard who had hijacked his palm receptor. He could always take a moment to access the personnel database, lock down the building. He could make demands of any Security Associate and they would be met immediately, without question. But that was probably what the terrorists were hoping for: Disruptive Incident at UniCorp HQ.

"Mr. Ambrose!" Danielson emerged from the other side of the fountain and handed him a small tan pellet. "Thought you might like a cup of tea before we went up. Lost each other in the great fleshbound shuffle, eh?" He winked as Ambrose swallowed the pellet. Immediate warmth spread from the center of his stomach, radiating out into his arms and legs. A slight peppermint aftertaste formed in his mouth. It was very good tea. He began to relax.

It was nagging him, though, that the guard had access to the kind of red-hot transfer that could override his receptors.

An unexpected override was a breach of professional etiquette, the kind of thing he would expect from Len, for whom everything was an urgent matter. But as he made his way across the lobby beneath the product of his family's peculiar genius, the shock of the renegade transmission faded to something distant and unimportant. He was a UniCorp Process Flow Team Leader, and there was the future of the company to consider. He approached the silver bullet-shaped elevator reserved for management-level Associates and flashed his palm. The door slid noiselessly aside.

"Good luck, sir," Danielson said. They shook hands, and Danielson repeated the company motto: "Better life in Unison."

"Better life in Unison," Ambrose said, watching the back of Danielson's head get smaller and eventually disappear as he melted back into the crowd.

Ambrose entered the plush cylinder and sat in the temperfoam armchair. He bobbed his head to the fractured beat of smooth techno. The elevator sped silently upward. He checked his face in the mirror and flashed his white teeth. He was about to be the youngest person ever to receive a Level Seven modification procedure. What made it a Level Seven, Ambrose knew, was that all subjects before him—hotshot businessmen, military personnel, civilian thrill seekers—had gone irreversibly insane within two weeks of the modification. Recorded results of this procedure included verbal and written incoherency, paranoia, self-mutilation, homicidal rage, vivid hallucinations, general dementia, and suicide.

What Ambrose also knew was that, as long as he obeyed the strict calibration regimen flowed out and finalized by his father and brother—a luxury not extended to the earlier recipients—he would maintain his present psychological state. A small amount of deviation was acceptable, as a lifetime without sleep was bound to have its unpredictable consequences. But the calibrations had a 99 percent success rate on the A.I. brain sims. And besides, innovation without risk defied the principles of UniCorp.

The elevator eased up at floor 350 and halted comfortably at 375. He took a deep breath and stood as the doors slid open to reveal a bare room the size of his closet. The walls were silver and seemed to swirl and drip like poured mercury. Occasionally, their color faded to a half transparency. He caught a glimpse of the hallway beyond and of the lab where the scan-tube awaited his arrival.

His older brother's disembodied voice said, "State your business."

Ambrose rolled his eyes. "It's me, Len. Who else could it be?"

"Observe protocol. State your business."

Ambrose sighed. His brother's smart-ass professionalism had become even more obnoxious in the weeks leading up to the procedure. He wondered if Len was jealous.

"Ambrose Truax, UniCorp Process Flow Team Leader. Here for scheduled Level Seven hypothalamus brain modification."

"Please enter the door at the other end of the hall."

"I know where I'm going, Len."

The flowing silver walls vapored into nonexistence. The white, windowless hallway glowed with filtered, reconstituted sunlight. Ambrose blinked and strode purposefully past a series of closed doors, which reminded him eerily of his recurring dream. *Your waking life is not your own . . .* He pushed the thought away and palmed open the door.

Inside the dim room, his brother stood before a monstrous externalized UniCorp data stream, a floating array of movable text and charts. Ambrose recognized part of it as the Process Flow he'd created with his father: the likelihood of every conceivable result of this operation. Success: 92 percent. Insanity: 1 percent. Suicide: 1 percent. And so on. Len flipped his palm and a detailed model of a human brain appeared in the air. Ambrose stepped inside, and the door slid closed behind him.

"Where's Dad?"

"Here, Ambrose, sorry." The deeply resonant voice came from a patch of faintly buzzing negative space that represented the thought patterns and personality of Martin Truax, who lived exclusively within Unison and projected himself into the real-world office for major events and board meetings. His flesh-bound self remained in permanent stasis in a location so secret not even his sons knew where it was.

"What's wrong?" asked Ambrose, struggling to focus on the blur.

"I'm having some bandwidth issues," his father explained, quivering slightly. "Had to fire Chen's team last night. Diverted some resources to fill the gap. The bulk of Unison remains unaffected, but a few backend problems have yet to be resolved."

Ambrose nodded, trying to picture Mr. Chen. Programming and Process Flow Associates rarely sought one another's company.

"I wanted him gone last year," Len said. "If you'd taken my advice, you could've saved—"

"Ah!" Tiny lines within the gray blur began to glow faintly like lightning inside a cloud. The lines connected and a human outline emerged. The room brightened as Martin Truax's projection revved up to 100 percent. Two previously unseen technicians appeared at the far end of the room, bustling around the gleaming scan-tube on its raised platform. Len vapored away his data stream and waited for the creator of Unison to finish arriving.

Their father was seventy-one years old but looked no older than forty. And it wasn't just a favorable projection: all his life, Martin Truax had taken advantage of the finest antiaging modifications that the world had to offer, traveling yearly to the Free Asian Union for rare, untested treatments. Ambrose watched as his father's sandy hair filled itself in. It always looked slept on, the direct opposite of the rest of his immaculate appearance: blue suit, maroon cuffs, gold UniCorp *U* stitched to the lapel.

The technicians at the other end of the room stopped and stared. Even projected, Martin Truax's kinetic force was impossible to resist. The man was a frayed wire of energy and ambition. Ambrose straightened his posture as the familiar mix of pride and anxiety washed over him.

Martin Truax smiled and extended a hand to his youngest son. Ambrose took it, and his palm receptors sent false sensations tingling up his arm. It felt just like shaking a human hand.

His father winked at him, then got down to business and began giving orders. The technicians scrambled. Ambrose followed his brother to the scan-tube, which slid open to reveal smooth, unbroken steel—except for one tiny hole for the microscalpel beam. Ambrose closed his eyes. His mouth was suddenly very dry. He had flowed out his possible nervous reaction many times, and knew with 100 percent certainty that he would get in the tube.

"Ambrose," Len said, surprisingly gently, "you won't feel a

thing. You know that." Len's eager blue eyes stopped their customary darting and gazed reassuringly at Ambrose, who nodded once. He looked back at his father, who was picking lines of code out of some externalized program file and replacing them with strings of glowing numbers from his palm. Len put a hand on Ambrose's shoulder.

"Consider this your promotion out of podcast squad."

Ambrose laughed. Sometimes Len could be okay.

"Problem?" his father called up from the floor.

Ambrose shook his head. It was time.

The next six hours passed like a fever dream. Inside the tube, he wasn't awake and he wasn't asleep. His body felt suspended within a vast empty space, even though it was lying supine in an area no bigger than half his bed. His mind never shut off completely, but he struggled to hold on to the basics of his life: the contents of his bedroom, the details of his job, his thousands of Friends in Unison. Eventually, he felt so disconnected that he had no choice but to stop thinking. His last thought before his mind blanked was that it was impossible not to think about *anything.*

When he was completely oblivious, the scalpel beam pierced his skull and brain stem. It tracked his hypothalamus and widened to envelop it completely. The beam sizzled through the membrane and vanished.

Modification.

Ambrose drifted lazily back to the surface of his thoughts. He felt spent and exhausted, like he could sleep for days. But of course he would never sleep again. Panic filled the space carved out by the beam. Something was wrong. He searched for the correct Process Flow to lead him to a comforting out-come, but there was nothing. Something had changed, some-thing he'd never planned for.

The transmission.

It had implanted part of itself before he'd deleted it, and now he was trapped inside the hardcoding. The woman with the accent had more to tell him, something elemental that couldn't be communicated until he was under the laser, recep-tors inside out. Something he wouldn't understand unless he was helpless to deny it and push it out of his mind. Her mes-sage was part of him, and he had no choice but to receive it.

Her message was his dream.

The familiar scene flooded back. A baby lay strapped inside a scan-tube. The lid opened and watery eyes focused on the world for the first time. Martin Truax, not a projection but fully human, shone a blue light up and down the tiny, squirming body. Technicians externalized charts.

His dream was a memory.

One of the technicians flipped a palm and the image of a baby appeared. Attached to the baby were dozens of metallic wires. The technician traced one with his finger, and Ambrose felt a prickly tingle in his arm. The wires were attached to his body. They were building him. He was the baby.

The memory was real.

He accepted this with no struggle or hesitation because part of him had always known it. Somehow the woman knew it, too.

He had never been born.

His closest relatives were the lab technicians who had cre-ated him.

Suddenly his brain abandoned the transmission, or the procedure abandoned his brain. Either way, the dream memory vanished.

They were pulling him out.

Created for what purpose? He strained to hold on to the transmission, but it was gone. Was that the end of the procedure, or were they panicking and yanking him out before he could learn the whole truth?

As the cold reality of the scan-tube leaked in, he once again became the sole inhabitant of his body.

The tube slid back to reveal the bare white ceiling of the lab.

"Ambrose." His father's voice.

"Don't try to sit up." His brother.

But he felt fine, if slightly groggy, as if he'd just woken up from a short, teeth-grinding nap. The top half of the tube tilted upright until he was face-to-face with his brother. His arms and legs were still strapped down. His feet rested on little platforms. Len smiled grimly.

"Congratulations, Ambrose."

Ambrose regarded his brother. As always, impossible to read. Had they become aware of the transmission? There was no way to find out. Best to keep his mouth shut. He tried to flow a quick process and realized how sluggish he was. He couldn't reach any real endpoint. The tube had opened into a new world with an unfamiliar set of possibilities and outcomes, and his ability was hopelessly scrambled. His heart hammered, but he kept his voice steady.

"How'd I do?"

"You didn't do anything except lie still inside the tube."

"I mean—"

"*We* successfully modified your hypothalamus and corresponding cephalic patterns. Your body's physical craving for sleep will no longer register."

"Get me out of this thing."

"You're aware that we have to run a series of tests, that you can't just—"

"Where's Dad?"

His father stepped into his line of sight. "As predicted, the procedure was a success. Len's going to run diagnostics, then we'll get you acclimated to the calibration process. Listen, son."

"Which?" Len asked.

"Ambrose."

"Can you undo these straps, please?" Ambrose asked.

His father ignored his request. "I want you to stay on task. You may think you feel fine, but it's important never to underestimate the psychological effects of a Level-Seven procedure."

Ambrose nodded curtly and slipped into the corporate-scientist-speak he used with his father. "We accounted for them in our initial Process Flow. Sixteen mid-spectrum outcomes involving extended dream states immediately following the procedure. My own internal monitoring indicates—"

Len scoffed. "How exactly are you performing this self-diagnostic? Checking for a sore throat?"

"Leonard," Martin said. Len busied himself with a series of slowly rotating externalized graphs. "Ambrose, what your brother's trying to say is that you need to relax and let us work."

"My endpoints are hazy. When will my Process Flow ability reconstitute?"

"Soon," his father assured him.

"You might feel a little pinch," Len said, placing his palms an inch from Ambrose's forehead and externalizing the data in the space between the tube and the ceiling.

"Shut up, Len."

Slowly, Len moved his palms around his brother's forehead and down along his face. Ambrose's feet twitched at the prickly sensation of almost-touch.

"Lemme see," he said. Len moved the data so that Ambrose could see the projection of his brain broken down into subsections and cross sections.

"See? I'm fine."

Len grunted. This wasn't exactly Ambrose's area of expertise. Len turned to the data, reached inside the hypothalamus, and expanded it by pulling apart. He poked deep into Ambrose's brain, and the memory of the transmission asserted itself. Ambrose's present reality was an imitation of his birth: projected brain activity, scan-tubes, Martin Truax. He studied his thought-pattern charts for some indication of what he was thinking. If Len and his father noticed anything, they kept quiet.

Suddenly his father glitched, vapored away. The lights in the room dimmed once again. Martin Truax sighed. "I'll maintain a vocal construct here in the lab. I'm not sure what's going on, but I can't seem to . . . Len, have Associates Billick and Greer shimmer into Unison Workspace after you're finished here. And the other one, there . . ."

Len cocked an eyebrow at the empty air. "Chen?"

"Chen."

"You *fired* Chen, sir."

"Well, see that he stays that way."

Len nodded. Ambrose squirmed against the straps on his wrists and ankles.

"Hey, I have to go to the bathroom."

"Hold it."

"Come on, I've been stuck inside the tube for—"

The straps popped open. Len glared at the empty air where their father had been.

"You've got enough data to get started, Len," his father's voice said. "And he'll be right back."

Ambrose hopped to his feet and kick-started his circulation.

"I'm proud of you," his father's voice said as he headed for the door. "And I love you very much."

Ambrose almost stopped completely. "Love you, too, Dad."

"Better life in Unison!" Len called after him as he palmed open the door and walked down the silent hallway to the elevator. He stepped inside and leaned close to the mirror, prodding his temples, his cheeks, the back of his neck. The procedure hadn't changed his outward appearance. He ran a hand along the top of his head, feeling for the slightest indication of the wires he'd been attached to as a baby. The memory had seemed so real inside the scan-tube. Why had he allowed a terrorist transmission to implant doubt on the most important day of his life?

"Destination, please," prompted the elevator.

He hesitated, trying to remember the last time his father had said "I love you."

"Executive bathroom," he said.

Ambrose gazed at his reflection and tried to imagine what it would be like to appear as a projected representation of himself. He realized for the first time how easy and natural it would be to lie if you were never truly face-to-face with anyone. How you might grow accustomed to it, being in the business of creating new and better worlds.

"Wait!" he said. "Lobby."

He was Ambrose Truax, the future of UniCorp. He had serious responsibilities. The course of his life had been carefully plotted. What was he doing, acting on impulse like this?

Immediately, he considered all the ways his father could track his movements: building surveillance, voiceprints, the transmitter and receptors in his own palm implants. He would have to be careful not to externalize any data in order to avoid the signal. That meant staying offline. And there was absolutely no way he could shimmer into Unison. The lack of Friend interaction was already nibbling at his brain. He fought a sudden, powerful urge to slap his palms together and shimmer in for a peek.

His heart was pounding. He closed his eyes and focused on the upward current in his gut as the elevator descended. Whatever he discovered, he would have to be back soon. There were calibrations to consider, his sanity to preserve. Some kind of explanation to give his father and brother.

The door slid open. He crossed the lobby, eyes down, trying not to think about the dozens of security scans he was passing through. At least it was still a mob scene. Outside the building, the bright morning had given way to a hot and hazy afternoon. The round-top articulated frame cars crowding the lower parking lot seemed to vibrate in the heat. Ambrose walked quickly, fighting the urge to flip his palm and summon a limousine service. Eventually he'd have to tap into the signal for geographic wikis or transit maps, but not this close to UniCorp HQ. What did average people do when they needed a ride somewhere in a hurry?

Taxi, he thought, looking around. He'd never been in one but was aware of the yellow cars that waited like vultures outside atmoscraper lobbies. He was nervous and flushed. His skinsuit excreted a sweat pellet, which dropped to the ground and rolled under a car. Next to that car was a decrepit taxi, one of those U-Space-era models that lacked the thrust vectoring to ride in the upper traffic streams. Well, that was okay. Little Saigon was down, not up.

He approached the faded banana yellow car. The driver was asleep in the front seat. He knocked on the window and the man woke with a start, spilling the coffee he clutched in his lap. The man turned to glare at Ambrose. The skin around his left eye, along with the eye itself, was gone, replaced by a plasteel graft that glinted in the afternoon sun.

The window slid open.

"Off-duty, kid," rasped the cabbie.

Ambrose couldn't look away. He'd never seen such a shoddy facial modification. Maybe it was the work of some illegal chop shop.

"It's—it's an emergency," Ambrose stammered.

The plasteel eye grew out from its socket, trailing a cord, and scanned Ambrose up and down. It hissed faintly, then returned to the cabbie's face.

The window began to shut. Ambrose looked over his shoulder. Another sweat pellet fell next to his foot.

"I can pay," he said. "I can pay whatever you want."

The window paused. The man ran his tongue around the space between his gums and lips so that the skin protruded. Then he spit into the empty coffee mug and stowed it under the dashboard. "Well, I'm about to go home, so if it's on the way, then . . ."

Ambrose pulled up the heavy door and slid into the back

seat. The door slammed shut. It smelled like synthetic pine and real tobacco.

"Little Saigon, please," Ambrose announced.

The cabbie burst into dry, phlegmy laughter.

Ambrose slid low in the seat. "Like I said, it's kind of an emergency, so if we could just—"

"Sure, kid. Sure." The cab lurched off the ground as the lifts sputtered and engaged. "You got friends there?"

"Something like that."

The cabbie shrugged, chuckling, and entered the ground-level ESC traffic flow. The pattern was perfectly arranged to be accident-free and efficient, so long as drivers relinquished control of their vehicle to the system. Failure to do so was grounds for loss of license and arrest.

This driver failed to do so with such nonchalance that Ambrose wondered how he kept his job. Then he realized there was no license displayed anywhere in the cab. He held on as the driver cut across four carefully controlled lanes and drifted halfway into a fifth before hitting a thruster-boost, rising up over the traffic and turning down a blind alley between two atmoscrapers. They popped out the other end, where the driver momentarily joined the orderly traffic, pulled another sideways maneuver, and screeched to a stop in front of a plexi cylinder the size of an elevator.

Subcanopy airlock.

"This one takes you to the edge of Little Saigon." The driver turned to face him, regarded Ambrose's blue holo-suit, his unblemished skin. "You sure about this, kid? I mean, I don't wanna poke my eye where it don't belong, but maybe you wanna get your kicks slummin' in some Unison dive instead of ol' Little S." The cabbie raised the eyebrow that was still attached to human skin. Ambrose calculated that if he turned around now, he could return to the lab with a minimum of awkward explanation.

Then he thought of his dream. He thought of the woman from the transmission and what else she might know.

"This is fine, thanks. How much do I owe you?"

"Just try not to die down there, and we'll call it even."

"You mean—"

"Get outta here." The back door opened.

"Thank you," Ambrose said.

The driver grinned. Most of his teeth were ruined stumps. "It was on my way home."

Ambrose hopped out of the cab. The street was mostly deserted. No one looked at him. Inside the airlock, he rode a rusty platform down past a plexi display case. He peered inside. Steam swirled around several bluish white statues. He looked closer and realized they were people frozen in openmouthed terror. He shuddered. Was this some kind of public art exhibit?

Then he remembered something his father had told him long ago: there was flash-coolant in the airlocks. Topside residents with hardcoded IDs could come and go as they pleased without triggering the coolant. But if unauthorized subcanopy dwellers tried to ascend, they'd find themselves trapped in the airtight chamber as first their internal organs froze, then their blood, then their skin.

And, his father had chuckled, if they were truly lucky, they'd find themselves displayed inside the case as a warning to their fellow citizens. If not, they'd simply be discarded.

It was an effective deterrent.

One of the icy figures was a teenage boy who'd put his hands in front of his face at the final moment. His wide eyes peered through splayed fingers. In front of him someone had scratched PEEK A BOO into the plexi.

What kind of a place was this?

The platform hit the bottom with a jarring thud. The airlock door slid upward. Steam escaped.

For the first time in his life, Ambrose Truax stepped out into the subcanopy streets.

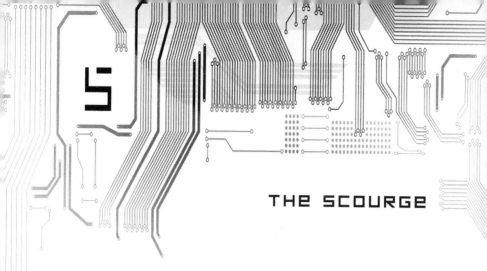

5

THE SCOURGE

"**YOUR NEIGHBORHOOD'S** different than I thought it would be," Ambrose said in the strained whisper he'd been using the entire time. "It's . . ." He tapped his knee, struggling to find the words. "I mean, as soon as I left the airlock, there was no way to find anything out. I guess I'm just used to accessing information, and down here it's like stepping into a time machine and going back a hundred years. I'm not trying to insult you; it's just—anyway, I don't know. I wandered around, and then your . . . friend Jiri grabbed me, and then a second later the cops were there, and then you."

Mistletoe kept her eyes closed. She didn't answer him. Ever since his description of the dream—*her* dream—his story had become a droning background to her own racing thoughts. If he was telling the truth, and the woman in his transmission was telling the truth, did it mean she wasn't real? Did it mean that she and Ambrose shared a common creator? She let go of his hand and rubbed the sides of her face where the dream wires had been. Smooth, unbumpy skin. Normal human features.

"It's not true," she said quietly.

"Sorry, I don't mean it's bad down here. I just mean it's . . . different."

"The message, I mean."

Ambrose didn't say anything. Even in the dark she could feel his halting explanation die on his lips. *He's not sure*, she thought.

"Maybe it just seems extra real because it was your very last dream ever or something."

"So you think I ran out on my life for no reason?" Ambrose said fiercely.

"Shhh!" she whispered. "I don't know. Doesn't seem like you do, either."

He lowered his voice to a hoarse whisper. "You have no idea what I just gave up."

During the silence that followed, she opened her mouth twice to tell him about her dream—the dream they shared—but something held her back. If Ambrose knew, they'd have to talk about it, and she wasn't ready for that. Instead she said, "That thing they did to you—"

"The hypothalamus modification?"

"Whatever. It'll make you, I mean . . . you'll never sleep again? Not ever? Just so you can work more?"

Ambrose took a deep breath, then let it out. Once again, she got the impression that he was struggling to communicate with someone he considered younger, even though they were the same age. She squeezed his hand tight to keep from strangling him.

"I have—" He stopped himself. "I *had* an enormous amount of responsibility. You could spend a lifetime trying to navigate UniCorp's infrastructure and never make it all the way through.

But imagine if you could take all the time you waste sleeping and actually apply it productively? The choice was simple."

"So it was something you loved," she said.

"What was?"

"The things you did, whatever they were. Process Flowing and all that. Your job."

She felt him shrug next to her in the dark. "It's who I am."

"Who you *were*," she reminded him.

"Maybe," he said quietly. "But you're right, I don't know." He wriggled his hand out of her grasp. She felt a twinge of disappointment as they broke contact, then silently scolded herself for caring.

"Sorry," she said. "I guess it's impossible to be completely, one hundred percent sure about something."

"Not for me it isn't," he said. "That's the point."

Next to her in the dark, Ambrose froze. She felt his body tense. He found her hand and squeezed it. She was glad to have it back.

"What?"

For a moment he sat coiled like a spring, then relaxed his grip.

"Thought I heard something," he said.

"There's nothing—"

A blinding green flash illuminated the floor, and for a brief moment she could see that they were not alone. Darkness returned. Two brilliant green spheres arced toward them, trailing white static.

"Run!" she screamed. She grabbed wildly for his flailing hand. One of the spheres surrounded her face before she could duck. She stood paralyzed, seeing only green. A low, rumbling frequency filled her ears and leveled off into a midrange hum. Her teeth chattered violently. Behind her ribs she felt a tiny internal separation, like a water-dipped finger breaking the surface and pulling away. Then her ears popped and the green sphere vanished. She crumpled to the floor, hoping with her final conscious thought that Ambrose had gotten away.

Sometime later, Mistletoe woke up on a musty pile of pillows and blankets. Her head was fuzzy, and she was very thirsty. She sat up slowly, blinking back a headache, and looked around. She was in a dim, windowless room cluttered with piles of serpentine cables and antennae. Nelson and Ambrose were gone. Instinctively, she patted herself down.

Body intact. Clothes on. Necklace in place.

She creaked to her feet like an old lady, steadying herself against the coiled guts of some boxy pre-Unison machine. There was a single metal door with a little peephole a few inches above her head. She walked over and jumped up, but the lens was for looking in and she couldn't see anything. She tried the doorknob.

It swung open.

Ma buh . . .

She blinked twice, scrunching her whole face up and rubbing her eyes to make sure she wasn't dreaming.

She was standing at the edge of a subterranean zoo. Far above her head, orange and blue birds darted in and out of strange formations. Ravens perched ominously on trapeze bars suspended from the domed ceiling. Beehives and nests of all different shapes and sizes were slung across thick branches. Beneath them, monkeys and chimpanzees swung lazily back and forth. A few feet in front of her, the gray cement floor gave way to a grassy plain where huge beasts covered in tangles of thick brown fur grazed. Beyond them, two goats locked horns on top of an enormous gray rock. The middle of the room was a pond where ducks and geese rested.

It was all completely silent.

Suddenly the room began to vibrate, then shake. Spooked birds left their perches in tight bunches as the ceiling rained bits of plaster. She lost her balance and tumbled onto the grass. It was the same deep rumble she'd heard on the thirtieth floor, except now she was closer to the source. Was the Scourge some kind of stampede? She curled up in the soft grass and covered her ears, trying to remember if there had been any elephants.

A second later the silence returned and she opened her eyes. The tallest man she had ever seen was standing over her. He had messy white hair, pale wrinkly skin, and a scrawny neck that looked a bit too long. He was wearing a drab gray robe that hung loosely from his body and clung to his ankles.

He smiled gently and extended a hand. She ignored the slender fingers, pushed herself to her feet, and backed away from him.

"We're glad to see you up and about, child," he said. His eyes radiated a penetrating brilliance that seemed at odds with his soothing voice. "And we apologize about your less-than-warm welcome, but I'm afraid we had no choice."

"What did you do to us? Where's Ambrose?"

He took a step toward her and stretched out his hand again. "Come, you can see for yourself."

She backed away once more. He nodded in understanding and folded his arms across his chest. Behind him, one of the brown furry beasts lumbered past, gave her a passing glance out of big black eyes, then bent to munch grass.

"The unpleasantness you experienced earlier was necessary to remove any implanted tracers."

Mistletoe remembered the internal pulling sensation and rubbed her chest. "We were bugged?"

"*He* was bugged, of course. You were not, but we had to be sure."

She nodded carefully. That explained how the cops had picked up Ambrose's trail as soon as he hit the subcanopy streets. She wondered if that was why his escape from the UniCorp building had been so easy: Martin Truax had wanted him to run so his men could follow. Ambrose was the bait, but for whom? Jiri and Aunt Dita?

She composed her face into a blank mask and clenched a tight fist at her side. "Who are you? What is this place? Where's Nelson?"

He furrowed his white eyebrows. "Nelson?"

"My scoot."

"Ahh, yes. Listen, I know I've given you no reason to trust me, but if you'll just follow, I promise to show you everything."

Mistletoe bit her lip. She supposed that if he wanted to kill her, he would have done it already, and if he meant her harm, he could have had his chance while she slept. She nodded. "Okay. But don't hold my hand. Ever."

He laughed. "Can we perhaps shake just once? My name is Magnus. This place is my home. Your vehicle is intact."

"No, we can't. My name's Mistletoe. Your home is friending *weird*, and Nelson *better* be safe."

Magnus shrugged and led her down the gently sloping

plain. They passed so close to the hulking brown animals that she expected to be overpowered by a beastly stench, but they didn't smell like anything. The whole place gave off a distant, musty odor like the pile of blankets she'd been sleeping on. It certainly didn't smell like a room packed with dozens of wild animals.

Near the pond they descended into a grassy trench that quickly became a cement tunnel. She glanced behind her as the magnificent room was eclipsed by brief darkness before they emerged into a much bigger tunnel. It was dim and damp and smelled like feet. Drops of water fell from corroded iron crossbeams above her head and plinked into shallow puddles.

"Step carefully, child," Magnus said, indicating the grid of steel bars laid out in regular intervals beneath her feet. "How much do you know about the history of your city?"

"I know about the Canopy Division Law and about the riots. I've never been down *here,* though. Before today I'd never even been inside the thirtieth floor. People go in, and they don't come out."

Magnus's eyes twinkled in the gloom. "Is that what they say?"

She nodded. "They say the Scourge gets them."

Maybe you feed them to the animals, she thought.

"Ah, yes. The Scourge." Magnus led her around one of the massive plasteel support beams that split the tunnel in half and burrowed into the ground. She followed him to the left, where a soft light cast long shadows on the decaying tile walls. Beneath the brown grime, she could make out a repeating pattern:

LEX 59 LEX 59 LEX

"We're in the old New York City subway system," Magnus explained. "The very bottom of ESC, forgotten by most, ignored by the rest. My brother and I have been here for quite some time."

She had heard of the old train tunnels, but it was common knowledge that the entrances and exits had been filled in long ago.

"The way is shut to everyone except my brother and me and a few others," he said. She wondered if he could read her thoughts. It wouldn't have surprised her.

They rounded a bend and the tunnel became fully illuminated. Here the grime had been scrubbed from the walls and the rails lining the floor tapered off into a smooth tile path. In front of her, bathed in the glow of an enormous chandelier, two leather couches flanked an iron door.

Magnus said, "Welcome to our home. In the past, some of our privileged guests have included your guardian, Jiri, and his sister, Dita."

Mistletoe stopped. His words created an immediate lump in her throat. She swallowed mightily and grabbed his sleeve, twisting the soft fabric in her hand. "You know Aunt Dita? Is she alive? Is she here?"

Magnus shook his head and pushed open the iron door. "We've lost contact," he said darkly. She dropped his sleeve and followed him into a brightly lit room about half the size of the silent zoo, cluttered with unwieldy pre-Unison computers and gleaming modern laboratory equipment that reminded her of her dream. The walls were lined with rows of open scan-tubes with tangles of machine guts spilling out. In front of her, Nelson was propped against a pile of familiar-looking plastic boxes. *Microwaves,* she thought. Jiri's shop had dozens. She wondered how long it would take her to sprint to Nelson, kick-start the engine, engage the lifts, and take off down the tunnel. She wished she knew how to use Ambrose's prediction-flow whatever-thing. Her best guess was that Magnus would grab her before she could reach the iron door, which had shut behind them anyway.

In the center of the room a tree trunk of thick wires descended from the ceiling and snaked along the floor like roots. The root wires branched off in various directions and attached to the hybrid machinery that lined the walls. Next to the base of the trunk stood an even older version of Magnus. His hair and skin had a decaying, yellowish tint. He wasn't quite as tall but was dressed in a similar gray robe. At his feet sat a big black labrador with what appeared to be the curved horns of a mountain goat protruding from its skull.

"My brother, Ivor," Magnus said. The goat-dog and the man glanced at her and gave simultaneous nods.

"Which one?" Mistletoe asked.

Magnus led her to the man. The goat-dog nuzzled her hand with its wet nose. Like the animals in the zoo, the dog was completely silent. She couldn't even hear it pant.

"*Carpe somnium,*" Magnus said. "Update?"

Ivor flicked his eyes at Mistletoe, then back to his brother. Ivor's eyes were flat and steely, in sharp contrast with Magnus's mischievous gleam. She couldn't decide which pair she liked least. When Ivor spoke, his voice was emotionless and distant, as if he were reporting on a topic that bored him.

"The initial ID wipe was not without its . . . difficulties." Another flick of his eyes indicated a bucket full of bloody rags.

"Young Truax is obviously hardcoded with the very latest UniCorp tags. And there is his recent Level Seven to consider. I've had to tread very lightly." He turned to a row of flat pre-Unison monitors and punched the keys of several keyboards at once.

Magnus turned to Mistletoe. "We do our best to stay up to date down here, but every UniCorp advance sets us further behind. There's too much technological ground to make up. You may want to cover your ears."

"My ears?"

Magnus grabbed her hands, slapped them over her ears, and held them in place. She squirmed for a moment, and then the deep rumbling began. It had been faint on the thirtieth floor and loud in the zoo, but in this room, at the source, it was unbearable. The vibrations entered her body through her nose and mouth. She sank to her knees, and Magnus knelt in front of her, clamping his hands tighter on her head. Her stomach twisted into a shaky knot. Her throat constricted, as if the immensity of the sound were wrapping around her neck. Her eyes blurred. As she struggled to suppress rising bile, the silence returned. Magnus helped her to her feet.

The two brothers and the dog had been completely unaffected by the deafening rumble. Ivor punched keys. The dog licked its front paws.

She took a few deep breaths, felt the noise leave her body in vibrating waves.

"The Scourge is this *room*?" she asked, her voice sounding distant and muffled. "People are just scared of the noise?"

"An unintentional bonus," Ivor said.

"We maintain the most sophisticated pirate signal—that

we know of—in the entire subcanopy community," Magnus explained. "It tests the limits of our equipment when we ask too much of it, and the equipment protests with its little . . . complaint."

"Give it some vegetable oil and a few hard kicks," she said, trying to organize her scattered thoughts into real questions. "So who are you? How do you know Jiri and Aunt Dita? Where's Ambrose?"

The brothers glanced at each other. Ivor shrugged mildly and disappeared around the side of the wire tree trunk, which was wider than her home on top of the shanty-stack. The goat-dog padded silently at his heels.

Magnus smiled at her again, or tried to. Since their meeting in the zoo, each subsequent smile had been a little less enthusiastic. Now he was down to a hard, thin line. In her head she counted the steps it would take to reach Nelson at a dead sprint.

"How much do you know about Unison?" he asked.

"Enough," she lied. The truth was, like most subcanopy residents, she didn't know very much at all.

Magnus arched his bushy white eyebrows and pursed his lips. Then he nodded slightly and said, "Hmm. Well, Ivor and I were part of the original UniCorp development team. We designed the framework for the Unison 2.0 upgrade, and then shortly after it went live, Martin Truax assigned us a highly classified new project. We were . . . very well paid for our work."

He spoke with barely disguised longing for what Mistletoe assumed was his old life topside. Around the other side of the wire trunk, something whirred to a clunky stop. Ivor swore.

"At first our instructions were vague," Magnus continued.

"Martin Truax was reluctant to share even the sketchiest clues about the purpose of our project. We were given coded transmissions and accompanying data that was meaningless and jumbled—we didn't know from where, or from whom—and told to decipher the content as best we could. When we complained, pointing out that knowledge of the transmissions' origin was vital to our task, Martin threatened to remove us from the project. The next day he changed his mind and admitted that the transmissions were from someplace within Unison."

Magnus began to wander the room as he talked, hands clasped behind his back like a gentleman taking a stroll in his garden. The skin around his eyes wrinkled and smoothed as he concentrated on his memories. Mistletoe followed warily as they moved farther away from Nelson.

"My brother and I decoded enough of the transmissions to realize that they may have been discovered within Unison, but they surely originated somewhere else. Unison was merely a communication tool for the senders. When we presented our findings to Martin, he was able to determine that the decoded transmissions composed a sort of . . ." Magnus trailed off and chewed his lower lip. "Instruction manual."

"For what?"

Mistletoe had forgotten all about Jiri and Aunt Dita, and the cops, and the silent zoo. She was thinking about the creation dream she shared with Ambrose. She had a horrible creeping notion that she knew the answer to her own question.

"A hybrid organism." Magnus coughed nervously. "Erm . . . *two* hybrid organisms, to be exact."

"Me and Ambrose." Her heart pounded. Her mind reeled.

Magnus stopped walking and regarded her with weary kindness. "Yes. That's right. The sender wanted us to build them . . . build *you*, that is."

She managed a faint "Who?"

"Ivor and I believe the sender is something close to *us*— that is, biologically close to human—but from another place entirely. Think of the universe as a great mansion with millions of rooms. Most of the time, the rooms on one end of the mansion are completely shut off from the rooms on the other end. But sometimes a tiny trapdoor opens, and something manages to sneak through. We believe the transmission was something like this and that Unison acted as the trapdoor."

Mistletoe's mouth was dry and sticky. She kept telling herself, *I am talking to the man who made me.* It didn't seem real. She felt like it was something she was supposed to find out many years from now, and that the world had made a huge mistake by giving up its secrets so soon.

"Why am I here, then?" Her voice was suddenly hoarse. "What did you make me for?"

Magnus's smile faded to the thinnest, hardest line yet. He touched her gently on the shoulder. This time, she didn't pull away. He opened his mouth and hesitated, glancing at his brother, who had appeared next to them wiping his hands on a bloodstained rag.

"We haven't the faintest idea," Ivor said, his monotone coated in bitterness. "Martin decided we knew too much about his precious secret project and had our UniCorp Admin privileges revoked. Then our employment was terminated. We figured it was only a matter of time before he had our throats cut, so we became ghosts. The reason for your existence is as much a mystery to us as it is to you." He lifted a slender hand to point back at the wire trunk. "But not for much longer."

The wires at the backside of the trunk were parted like curtains. Inside stood Ambrose, palms flipped up and suspended by small hammocks made of thin silver fibers that disappeared up the center of the trunk. His hands were bandaged. All around him, externalized information danced in the air. Ambrose stared out unblinking from the pulsing, strobing bursts of color at the source of the signal. He was standing on his own, but his eyes were glassy and unseeing.

Mistletoe turned back to Ivor, who was now holding a police stunner baton like the one Red had used in the streets of Little Saigon. Behind him, Magnus studied the floor.

"We're going to have to ask you to join him, Anna," Ivor said.

"That's not my friending *name*!" she screamed.

The deep rumbling of the Scourge drowned her out.

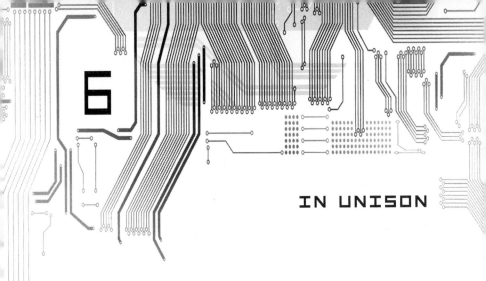

6

IN UNISON

Nᴇᴡ ᴜsᴇʀ.

Ambrose focused on these two words like they were a cherished memory. Anticipation burned hot and sweet within him. He loved Unison, despite the circumstances. He would always love Unison. It wasn't tedious to build a new Account from scratch; it was wonderful. The throbbing in his palms where Ivor had rebooted his receptor implants dulled to a slight ache.

All around him, the signal core rumbled.

He tasted battery acid, endured the familiar symptoms of the shimmer, and emerged topside into a bright, perfectly calibrated Unison morning. Subcanopy ESC had never been bitmapped for insertion, so he was most likely directly above the brothers' subway-tunnel home.

The entire city was silent and empty. As a new user, he had no Friends. Bland, colorless atmoscrapers loomed above him. His footsteps echoed as he walked past blank storefronts and stately corporate lobbies. The air smelled faintly of rice. He remembered Associate Garvey's programming team arguing for weeks about the exact specifications of the new user smell.

After a long moment of contemplation—Unison would never look or feel this peaceful again—Ambrose accessed his Profile. The mirror appeared in his mind, splitting his perception of Unison into two distinct areas: the empty city around him that he could touch and smell, and the details of his new Account. He was suddenly able to sense aspects of the new personality that Ivor had implanted to avoid detection by UniCorp scans. Hopefully this mask would prove useful. He turned the mirror inward.

He was Adam Trevor, an aspiring pop singer in search of his big break. His interests included twenty-first-century music, furniture design, and apple picking in the New England Expansion.

Okay.

He chose to make this information public and tasted a hint of battery acid again. All around him, the city began to change. The faint rice smell became starchier and somehow *closer*, as if it were cooking nearby. Beneath his feet, the sidewalk rippled. Gnarled roots emerged, pushing the pavement aside. Dozens of tiny saplings sprouted from the bed of roots and rose past his knees. White petals popped open and blossomed radiantly before drifting to the ground, where they covered the patches of pavement that hadn't been replaced by soft grass.

Ambrose walked between the thickening trunks as their branches stretched above his head. All at once, millions of green leaves sprang forth and quivered gently in an unfelt breeze. The noise—a faint rustling—sounded wrong. Too tinny and sharp. Ambrose made a note to forward the error to a Design Associate, then remembered that he no longer had access to his Admin Deck. He would have to ignore any system bugs he stumbled across. But maybe the rustling noise was specifically designed for Adam Trevor's ears? This new ID was going to take some getting used to.

He stopped, closed his eyes, and took a deep breath. The rice smell had been replaced by something rich, sweet, and comforting. He snapped open his eyes to find that he was standing in the middle of a fully formed orchard. Through gaps in the overlapping leaves, he could see splotches of gray and blue, city and sky. Ripe red apples dangled from trees in clumps, in pairs, alone. He reached up, grabbed one of the loners, and yanked. The branch bowed and catapulted up as the apple popped free. He took a bite. Juice ran down his chin. It was perfectly delicious, even tastier than a BetterApple. There really was no substitute for expertly calibrated Unison food. Munching greedily, he made his way to the edge of the orchard and dropped the core into a pile of white petals.

He left the shade of the last tree and stepped out onto the sidewalk. The city had gained in population: thousands of potential Friends—users with similar interests and values and thought patterns—appeared as translucent ghosts walking the streets. He moved among them slowly, unused to the anonymity the new ID provided him. There were no attempts to mass-Friend him. No Application creators were mobbing him for approval. He watched a vaporous little boy chase an even younger Friend across the street. Under the UniCorp Family Plan, even infants could be granted a login. Their privileges were severely limited, but it was in UniCorp's interest to create the demand for BetterLife as early as possible. Status-conscious parents tended to have reckless spending habits.

A Feed that occupied the same internal mirror space as his Profile blinked to life.

Ambrose Truax @ New User Adam Trevor: On behalf of my family, I'd like to extend a very warm welcome. Better life in Unison!

Shocked, Ambrose almost shimmered out before he remembered that Len had insisted on sending automated "personal" messages to each new user. There was one from Len, one from Ambrose, and one from their father.

He remembered the day he had argued with his brother about the wording of the welcome message. Such a pointless, trivial detail, and yet they had spent hours going back and forth. He squinted up at the geometric patches of blue sky that appeared between the atmoscrapers. Barely any time had passed since he had run out on his old life, and already the things he used to care about seemed absurd. Then suddenly the details of his bedroom came rushing back—closet full of holo-fashion, top-of-the-line synth-table, beautiful view of the pasture building next door—and a dull ache spread from his chest to his legs.

He'd never see those things again.

Clamping down on the wave of longing, he reminded himself that Ambrose Truax's family, career, and possessions were all built upon the great lie of his creation and that he was here in Unison to find the truth. Magnus and Ivor had shown him the classified transmissions. He knew his father's secret: along with Mistletoe, Ambrose had been created according to the transmission's instructions. This was an unreal, disconnected sort of knowledge. He didn't *feel* any different, but then again, he hadn't yet viewed the specific blueprints of his creation. It was hard enough to grasp the fact that he wasn't fully human; he didn't need to see the spidery nanotech of his cellular makeup laid out coldly before him. There would be time, later, for such strange and painful things.

First, he had accepted the brothers' offer to help track down and pinpoint the source of his creation instructions. He didn't exactly trust the brothers and their anti-UniCorp friends, but Magnus had posed an irresistible question: *How many people in this world get to personally investigate the mystery of their own existence?*

Not very many, Ambrose had conceded. Maybe he was the only one.

His Feed continued:

UniCorp Presents: Maximize Your Happiness! Stay in BetterLife longer, expand your Friendships, and achieve your goals with a revolutionary new outpatient procedure. Ask us how!

For each item he absorbed, his immediate *like* or *dislike* reaction was measured and recorded. A UniCorp Process Flow team had created a template for Adam Trevor's personality type and would scramble to fill in the blanks as they received more information. It was usually pleasant to be in a world where things simply fell into place, but inhabiting Adam Trevor's Unison Account was slightly unsettling. The comforting, womblike experience he'd spent his life working to maintain and improve felt off-kilter, as if he'd awakened into someone else's dream.

A boy appeared before Ambrose on the sidewalk. Unlike

the other ghosts, he was fully fleshed out. His shiny black hair flopped over his eyes, and he regarded Ambrose with a mixture of interest and amusement. The boy held out his hand. Ambrose smiled and took it. When their palms touched, a rush of Profile information invaded his Feed.

He had been assigned his First Friend.

Takashi Nakamura was sixteen. He shared Adam Trevor's interest in twenty-first-century music. Additionally, they were both confident but accident-prone, allergic to mildew, and broke out into horrible sweats when talking to girls.

Of course, Takashi's Profile could be a complete fabrication, just like his own. For all Ambrose knew, Takashi could be a billionaire trust-fund prince from the North Pole.

Or a UniCorp Associate.

"Hey," Takashi said, lowering his hand and nodding curtly. "Welcome to BetterLife."

Ambrose understood that Takashi had 42,578 Friends and spent most of his in-Unison time hanging around the Mass Entertainment Immersion Center.

"How was your first shimmer?" Takashi asked, grinning.

"Kinda weird," Ambrose said, playing the part of a new user. "Tasted bad."

"That's what BetterMints are for, twitterbrain. So what took you so long? Parents wouldn't let you join the party? You religious or something?"

"We just got the money for a login ID. My dad got a new job. Before that we lived—" He almost said *subcanopy*, but stopped himself. "Anyway, it was my birthday present."

"Happy birthday, pop star. We got a lot to celebrate!"

"We do?"

"I've never been a First Friend before!" Takashi was ecstatic. His Mood-shadow, one of the more popular Unison Applications, began to dance on the ground beneath his feet. Ambrose laughed. By appreciating the Mood-shadow, he'd invited Application offers into his Feed:

Too many Events to attend? Feeling overwhelmed? Fake your own Account deletion with UniGone!

Mood-shadows are great, but are they Workspace-appropriate? Tone it down with a Mood-tooth. 100% fun, 0% distraction.

And he received his first Thoughtstream update, which felt like a faint fingertip caress behind his eyes:

Takashi Nakamura **thinks Adam Trevor is about to have the best birthday ever.**

"Um . . . ," Ambrose said. "I don't have any plans, or anything."

"You do now," Takashi said. "Come on." He beckoned for Ambrose to follow him through the ghost-crowd. Ambrose hesitated.

"I'm waiting for someone."

"Nice try. I'm your only Friend, remember?" Takashi's Mood-shadow crossed its arms. Ambrose had to wait for Mistletoe in the same place he'd shimmered into. Ivor had promised she'd be inserted as soon as she woke up, and he couldn't keep tabs on her until they were Friends.

All around him, Unison kept changing.

The atmoscraper to the left was bright green—Adam Trevor's favorite color. The imposing white marble lobby was replaced by a cluttered vintage record and clothing store. The huge mirrored-glass doors were covered in tattered posters of bands Ambrose had never heard of. A slight coating of grime appeared on the streets, and bits of trash collected along the curb. Adam Trevor favored a gritty urban environment. Inwardly, Ambrose shuddered. Why would anyone make their Unison experience *dirty*? But at least it reassured him that Ivor's implants were working. So far, the UniCorp scans were responding only to Adam Trevor's supposed reactions and desires.

"Hey, pop star," Takashi said impatiently. His Mood-shadow boxed the air. "You coming, or what?"

Down the street, an open-air arcade appeared. Rows of ancient console games sprang to life, their graphics perfect and glitch-free.

"I really don't think I can. Like I said, I'm—"

"Waiting on a mysterious friend. I heard you." The Mood-shadow hung its head.

Ambrose tried his best to look apologetic. "Sorry—maybe some other time?"

Takashi Nakamura thinks his new Friend hates fun or something.

Ambrose looked down at his shiny, checkered shoes. He felt his new Friend's disappointment as his own: a letdown sharp and abrupt and tinged with a surprising amount of sadness. *Takashi is lonely,* he realized. And with this realization came the understanding that Takashi knew that Ambrose knew he was lonely. Their Thoughtstreams had meshed. Ambrose hoped that Ivor's new implants were good enough to keep his own basic and uninformative. His Feed said:

Play Saturn Moon Wargames now! First 500 users get free pulse disruptor upgrade!

He thought briefly that it couldn't hurt to relax and have a little fun. The past twenty-four hours had been stressful, and if he let himself fully accept the Adam Trevor ID, Unison would take care of all his decisions. He could float leisurely from one distraction to another.

Takashi's Mood-shadow perked up, responding to this hopeful train of thought. Ambrose felt openhearted. He felt like being recklessly generous. He felt like he'd known Takashi forever. The adrenaline rush of the First Friend connection was something he hadn't experienced in a very long time. If he just let go and followed Takashi, he could sustain the buzz and, with each new Friend, build upon their collective Thoughtstream.

Except now, he reminded himself, he had a purpose in life—a mission—that wasn't based on a lie. And people were counting on him. It didn't take much to get sidetracked in this place.

Focus, Ambrose.

He figured any detective had to begin with the right set of questions. And without his Admin Deck, questions were all he had.

"Hey, Takashi," he said, "how does this place work?"

"There's a tutorial. If you want, I can show you where—"

"No, I mean, how does it *really* work?"

Takashi narrowed his eyes. His Mood-shadow shrugged. "I don't know what you mean."

Ambrose nodded. He had to be careful. He glanced around. A mangy brown dog nosed in the gutter.

"Like that," he said, pointing. "That's my dog, right? They made it for me. So do you see a dog?"

Takashi nodded. "The overlap between Friends' perceptions isn't quite real-time, but it's close. They say Version 3.0's gonna have this stuff perfect."

"So you don't see a cat or an elephant or anything? You see the dog, too?"

"Yeah, but the question is, what color is it?" Takashi grinned. "What breed?"

"I don't know, um—golden retriever, I think."

Takashi cocked his head and said, "Hmm."

Takashi Nakamura just found out he prefers bulldogs.

"Right," Ambrose said. "Okay. But is there somebody I can talk to who knows how Unison makes the dog I see different from the dog you see?"

Takashi laughed. "You mean a Programming Associate? You just *got* here, Adam. No offense, but you're nobody. There's, like, two billion people ahead of you."

"No, I don't mean a real-life programmer. I just mean . . . somebody who . . . knows things." Ambrose winced. He was going to have to get better at this.

They watched the dog munch a ragged hunk of rawhide. Ghosts paraded past.

"Well," Takashi said thoughtfully, "I have a Friend you could meet, I guess."

Was it Ambrose's imagination, or had something changed between them? Takashi's energetic amusement had become shaded with caution. His Mood-shadow froze in place and quivered slightly.

Takashi Nakamura recommends a Friend: Sonia Carter.

A glimpse of Sonia Carter's Profile invaded his Feed. Fifteen years old. Ex-hacker turned authorized independent Application developer. Creator of UniPetz, the hassle-free, customizable animal companion service. He thought of Lincoln.

"Well . . . okay," Ambrose said, faking shyness. "I guess I should meet some more people anyway, huh?"

"That's the point," Takashi said. "Otherwise you'll never be anything in here. You'll just be . . . you."

Ambrose scanned the ghostly crowd for someone he could identify as Mistletoe. Magnus and Ivor had promised she'd be right behind him.

Takashi grabbed his arm. "We gotta go to the MEIC."

"The meek?" Ambrose played dumb.

"*M-E-I-C.* Mass Entertainment Immersion Center. That's where I met Sonia. She's always there."

Ambrose looked around. Again he longed for his Admin Deck. A simple crowd-sort and he could narrow the search by thousands. He should've given Magnus and Ivor more specific instructions for finding Mistletoe, but in the rush of new information, it hadn't occurred to him.

"Okay, but . . . my friend is new, like me. She won't know—"

Takashi grinned. His Mood-shadow threw back its head and laughed noiselessly. "Ahh, so the mysterious friend is a *female.* Listen, when you meet Sonia, you'll forget all about her. Trust me."

Ambrose thought for a moment. For all he knew, Mistletoe might still be sleeping off the effects of the tracer removal. He couldn't wait around forever.

He nodded to Takashi, who spun on his heels and led him in the direction of the arcade. As Ambrose passed through the crowd of ghosts, Profile information flooded his Feed. Thought-streams chattered. Billions of microblogged emotions—the fleeting joys and heartbreaks of daily life—skimmed just beyond his understanding like tiny fish scattering before an oncoming shark. A never-ending broadcast cycle of human connection, and he was missing it! Right now, *something* interesting or hilarious or poignant was being fed into the stream by one of his potential Friends on this very street, and all he could hear was a dull murmur. He followed Takashi past a gathering of translucent men sitting on an old-fashioned stoop. All around him the ghostly parade continued uninterrupted. So many users, and this was just one tiny segment of the logged-in population. He could spend a dozen lifetimes here and never meet them all. There would always be something happening that excluded him. Permanent insertion began to sound reasonable. Why not just stay? He could make millions of new Friends and forget all about his father, his brother, Magnus, Ivor.

He could forget about Ambrose.

He stopped and stared straight up. The top of a brilliant white atmoscraper sliced a crisp right angle into unbroken blue sky. He recognized the familiar sharpness of the edges, the seeming lack of distance between himself and the end of the block, between earth and sky. There was no haze, only 20/20 perfection and the clear-eyed comfort of coming home after a long day. He took a deep breath: the air smelled like clean sheets. He knew that Takashi could springboard him into hundreds of Friendship threads, and from there, thousands, millions, billions. He took another breath and let it out. With some difficulty, he dismissed the thought and focused on keeping up with Takashi.

Behind them, the dog threaded its way between the ghosts, nose to the sidewalk, following their scent.

FLIGHT OF THE CLOUD CHILDREN

MISTLETOE BIT the side of her tongue as the rumble of the Scourge chattered her teeth. She tasted rusty blood.

Run, she thought. But the vibrations in the room, her head, her belly rooted her to the floor like the wire tree trunk that held Ambrose. Knowing what to expect didn't make the noise any more bearable. She squeezed her eyes shut, clenched her teeth, and fought the frightening urge to jam her fingers right through her ears and into the middle of her head. Instead she sealed her ears shut with her palms until stillness returned to the subway tunnels and the last of the aftershocks melted away.

She opened her eyes.

The two brothers were frozen in place and waiting patiently for her to recover. Ivor extended the police stunner toward her casually, as if he were passing a baton in a relay race. Somewhere behind her, Nelson leaned against the pile of microwaves. How far? The Scourge had jiggled her bearings. She flicked her eyes from the tiny prism at the tip of the stunner to a brown mole alongside Ivor's nose to the downcast eyes of his brother, who seemed to shrivel under her glare.

She spit a mouthful of blood. Ivor watched it splatter on the ground between them. The black dog trotted to the red stain, lowered its horned head, and sniffed. She glanced at Ambrose, whose glassy, unseeing eyes reminded her of the antique Cabbage Patch doll in the back of Jiri's shop.

"What did you do to him?"

"It looks more dramatic than it actually is, Anna," Magnus said, abruptly resurrecting his kindly-old-man smile.

Her right hand clenched involuntarily at her side.

"Wiped his old ID," Ivor said. "New implants, new hard-coding. Basic new-user package. In Unison, he's unrecognizable as Ambrose. Now, if you'll be so kind, I need you to step over here." Ivor gestured with the baton toward the row of keyboards.

"Give him back."

Ivor shook his head. "I'm afraid he doesn't belong to you."

"I found him."

"I was present during his initial design phase."

"Ivor," Magnus said, "this child's just been through so much. For you to stand there and—"

Ivor's raised hand silenced his brother. A thin-lipped smile flashed across his face. "My brother is concerned with our image," he explained. "How we're perceived is regrettably more important to him than the urgent business at hand: figuring out what you and your much-better-behaved friend were created for in the first place, before Martin Truax hunts us all down like dogs."

"I'm not your creation," she said. The idea of these old men putting their wrinkly hands all over her infant self made her sick.

Ivor shrugged. He didn't seem to care what she believed. And he certainly didn't care if this was difficult or painful for her. At least Magnus had tried to smooth the transition. But had he been kind so she'd be easier to steer into a trap?

"Your other half is waiting," Ivor said.

"What my brother means to say," Magnus offered, "is that without you and Ambrose *together* in Unison, we believe our little"—he glanced at Ivor—"*your* bit of self-discovery will be impossible."

"Too bad," Mistletoe said.

Ivor pointed the stunner at her face.

Magnus sighed. "My brother and I, we're not . . ." He let out a dry, nervous chuckle. "This"—he indicated the bloody rags, the stunner—"is not how we are."

"Yes," Ivor said blandly. "This place is actually a soup kitchen." He clenched his jaw and squinted his eyes—an amateur's holo-dice bluff—and Mistletoe realized how unsuited to weaponry he was. Her street instincts screamed *Dive!*

The stunner extended in segments that flashed just above her head. Her right hand slid through her little puddle of bloody spit. The segments retracted back into the baton.

"Ivor!"

She glanced up in time to see Magnus throw himself in front of his brother as the stunner flashed a second time. Magnus crumpled instantly to his knees, head bowed, hands clasped behind his back, awaiting the cold cuffs of an ESC riot cop. Ivor lowered the stunner and blinked in surprise.

"Magnus . . ."

He stared blankly at the baton as if there were a button to reverse the effects. Mistletoe knew he would just have to wait, maybe hours if the stunner was high-grade. She sprang from the floor and charged toward Ivor, who fumbled to point the baton.

Too late.

She planted her left foot and delivered a Nelson-starting kick to Ivor's shin with her right. At the last second, she remembered she was wearing vintage steel-toed boots from Jiri's shop and felt a twinge of regret. Ivor looked, for the first time, like an old, frail, broken man. The kick spun him sideways. As her momentum carried her past, she caught the shock in his eyes.

The stunner clattered to the floor. She kicked it behind a row of scan-tubes.

"Sorry," she yelled over her shoulder as she turned to sprint toward Nelson.

She was halfway there when the black goat-dog emerged from behind a mess of wires and skidded into her path, toenails clacking against the hard ground, the stunner clenched in its jaws. A thick string of slobber dangled from the end of the weapon.

Mistletoe stopped. The dog seemed bigger now as it grinned at her, baring a row of teeth that stretched impossibly far back into its skull. It cocked its head to the side and looked at her quizzically. She swallowed. The only dogs she knew were the mangy vagrants that roamed the subcanopy streets, more scared of her than she was of them. This was something else— she wasn't even sure it was a dog.

Behind her, Ivor groaned in pain.

The goat-dog dropped the slick baton between its front paws. It twitched once, twice—and growled. Mistletoe's pigtail bristled down the back of her neck. She swallowed dry air. The goat-dog advanced cautiously, poised to leap. She glanced longingly at Nelson. So close. The goat-dog's hair stood up in a spiky wave along its back. Mistletoe wondered if it would go right for her throat and how, exactly, that would feel.

"Patricia!" Ivor's voice behind her said sharply. "Sit!"

Instantly, the creature's ears perked up like eager periscopes. Mistletoe thought, *Patricia?* The goat-dog sat on her haunches and panted expectantly.

"Stay!"

She turned around. Ivor was sitting on the ground, hugging his knee to his chest, glaring at her. Magnus knelt beside him, completely still.

Mistletoe didn't know what to say. *Thanks* seemed horribly inappropriate. She nodded at Ambrose, who remained suspended in the middle of the wire trunk.

"I'm taking him with me. How do I get him out?"

"You don't," Ivor said bitterly, rubbing his shin. "Of course," he added, "you can do what you want—I suppose I can't stop you. But if you disrupt his login externally, with the fresh hardcoding still raw and exposed, I can't guarantee his safety."

Mistletoe chewed her lip. She looked past the free-floating externalized data, the color fields and text blocks, into Ambrose's wide-open Cabbage Patch eyes. There was a chance that Ivor was bluffing, that if she ripped Ambrose away from the wire trunk, he'd wake up and be fine and they'd escape together.

"Mild disorientation is one possibility," Ivor said. "Severe damage to the frontal lobe is another."

She didn't want to take the chance. But if she left Ambrose here, where would she go? She watched the old man examine his leg. To keep from feeling sorry for him, she reminded herself that he'd ordered her around like she were nothing but a mindless cog in his personal machinery of revenge against Martin Truax. She decided that she would be better off figuring things out on her own, even if it meant leaving Ambrose—for now.

Without another word, she walked briskly toward Nelson, gingerly patting the soft fur atop Patricia's head between her horns. She scooped up the sticky baton, made a face, and carried it between her thumb and forefinger.

"You've made your point, Anna!" Ivor called after her. "Now listen to me: you're making a mistake!"

She pulled the scoot's handlebar free of the microwave pile and wedged the stunner into the tiny compartment beneath the seat.

"Don't be stupid," Ivor continued. "They'll hunt you down, be sure of that. You think Martin Truax will simply let this go? You and Ambrose are his prized experiments. *He will never rest.*"

She kick-started the scoot.

"You're throwing away your only chance! When he finds you, he'll—"

The engine sputtered and revved, drowning him out. The cushion of energy expanded beneath her. Nelson smelled like her musty old shanty, like roasting street meat, like a thousand close calls and tiny scrapes. Nelson smelled like home. She sped past the long rows of pre-Unison machinery, hopped off to open the iron door, and shot a glance back to the wire trunk, haunted by the secret life she shared with the boy she was leaving behind.

Back on the scoot, she crept through the living-room glow

of the brothers' hallway and into the dim, sour-smelling train tunnel. Nelson responded to the tracks with rattling bounces before smoothing out. She brightened the headlight and stalled, surprised. The tunnel was much wider than she thought. The tracks were just one of several sets that ran parallel in places and split off in others, descending into darkness. Each track was separated by a series of vertical beams like the hallways of a half-finished building.

She had no idea how to get back to the silent zoo. Little Saigon seemed impossibly far. She was about to pick a track at random when a gentle and expansive rustling sound caught her attention. She eased off the throttle and cupped her hands behind her ears to form little noise catchers. The rustling was louder now, an unseen thing headed straight for her. Bending forward, she pressed her chin against the handlebar and flattened herself against the scoot, just in time for the mad rush to come screaming out of the darkness.

Bats, she thought, but as the first bunch flapped chaotically past, she saw that they were tiny white birds no bigger than her hand. They swirled in clusters while solo birds orbited like electrons, thousands of them surging forward through the musty air above her head. Mistletoe wrinkled her nose at the feet smell they dislodged from the upper air of the tunnel. She held her breath and watched, fascinated, as one of the birds lost its aerial balance and spiraled down through the beam of Nelson's headlight to land on the tracks in front of her.

The little creature was covered in immaculately groomed white feathers, except for a tiny smudge of red between its eyes, which ran down the front of its white beak and ended in a sharp black point. It peeked up at Mistletoe (she could have sworn she saw it squint in the glare), jiggled its head, opened its beak, gave a tiny *cheweeep!* and flapped back up into the jet stream with the others.

Mistletoe had seen birds like these once before, years ago, on a trip to the New Egyptian Market. They'd been clustering madly in an ornate, gold-flecked cage hung from the back of a cart that sold exotic pets, high-grade absynthium, and reformatted cell phones. Mistletoe and Dita had been walking forever, just looking, ignoring the urging of the peddlers and the insistent haggling of shoppers. Dita wore a long yellow scarf wrapped several times around her neck and shoulders, and Mistletoe held on to the low-hanging end of the thin fabric, rubbing it absently between her fingers as they strolled.

Anna, Dita said, pointing to the cage.

What are they?

Chmura Dité, my mother used to call them. Cloud Children. See how they make a little group? Only by flying together as one do they move forward.

Anna looked up at Dita, who was watching the short, round man in charge of the cart argue with an unsteady couple about the price of absynthium. Instinct told her to drop her end of the scarf as Dita slid behind the cage and positioned herself between the birds and the little red-faced man. Something flashed from Dita's pocket, carving a blinding white arc through the air. She glanced back at Anna and gave a slight nod toward the other end of the market, then ducked into the crowd. But Anna stood, transfixed, as one side of the cage melted and pooled on the ground before hardening into a lumpy golden pretzel. The birds fluttered away through the hole, clustering and scattering above the crowd, fleeing, like Aunt Dita, toward the far end of the market. The little man squealed. Anna ran. When she finally snatched hold of the yellow scarf again, Dita turned to her, unsmiling.

Some things should never be for sale.

In the tunnel, Mistletoe wondered if these Chmura Dité were the offspring of that cluster Dita had freed or the creation of Magnus and Ivor. *Either way,* she thought, *they're headed out. What kind of bird wants to be trapped underground?* She spun Nelson and followed the birds up a gradually ascending tunnel.

After a while, she noticed she was rubbing the warm metal handlebar between her thumb and forefinger as if it were Dita's scarf. She blinked back tears. Support beams flew past like empty doorjambs. A thought, jumbled and dark, formed in the wake of the market memory: Aunt Dita knew what Magnus and Ivor knew, and she had kept it a secret for Mistletoe's entire life. So did Jiri, which meant there was one perfect starting place for her investigation: Jiri's junk shop, cluttered with relics of the past—and maybe some clues to her own.

Anyway, she would need better weapons.

When the Chmura Dité began to flap less erratically, their clusters slowed and joined into one dense cloud. Mistletoe sensed a new coolness in the air. On either side of her, the support beams were replaced by solid walls. The tunnel steepened. The Chmura Dité raced headlong toward two horizontal lights in the wall where the tunnel dead-ended. She slowed her approach and watched, puzzled, as the lights began to swallow them up. Not lights, she realized—exits. When the stragglers vanished, she crept forward to peer through the holes. There wasn't much of a view: the tunnel emptied into the bottom of an airshaft. It was impossible to tell if she was in Little Saigon or some other neighborhood, but at least it was outside. And the slits themselves were certainly big enough for her to crawl through. Problem was, with Nelson she'd be cutting it close.

But she couldn't just leave him.

She backed up and revved the scoot.

"Okay, Nelson. Sorry about this."

She gunned it, kept the nose down, and aimed for the bottom slit. Time slowed. *Believe,* she thought. At the last second before her head smashed the wall, she threw her weight down and back, pulling the handlebar with all her strength and pointing the lifts toward the opening. She disengaged them as she slid sideways through the hole.

The handlebar scraped the sides, shrieking.

She closed her eyes.

When the tunnel spit her out, Nelson spun from her grasp and she sprawled out on the garbage-strewn floor of the airshaft. She cringed as Nelson slammed into the opposite wall beneath a boarded-up window.

She caught her breath and tested her limbs: nothing broken.

Her heart was pounding as she waded through knee-deep trash to examine her scoot. A sickly sweet rotten fruit odor made her eyes water.

The ends of the handlebar were raw and jagged. The tailpipe was bent and slightly flattened. There was a thin scrape in the seat where a bluish gel oozed out. Temperfoam innards? Hyperlift juice? She didn't know and hoped it wasn't important.

She righted the scoot and sat down. She got her bearings: four brick walls rising straight up with makeshift balconies—wide planks stretching from one open window to another—crisscrossing until they overlapped to block her view. Lamps dangled from the planks, casting long, oval shadows down the walls and spotlighting sections of the garbage pile.

She knocked on the board covering the lowest window. It was pulpy and rotted.

"Sorry again," she said, and gave Nelson a swift kick start. He jolted once, then sped forward, splintering the board nose first.

She was once again inside the empty foundation of an atmoscraper. She weaved through the plasteel beams, hopped Nelson through an open window, and emerged into the diffuse glow of a subcanopy evening. It smelled like cheap cigars and humid sweat.

An hour later she ditched him in the dark space beneath an abandoned shanty's porch. She popped off her riding goggles—they tugged at the skin around her eyes—and hung them from the handlebar. She hated leaving Nelson alone and unattended, but she didn't want to come screaming toward the junk shop, which was most likely being watched. As an afterthought, she tapped open the compartment and grabbed the stunner, sliding it up her sleeve.

She made her way down a winding road, past a silent procession of black-robed monks. The junk shop was just down the block, sandwiched between a hair salon for old ladies and a long-defunct florist with a faded bonsai tree ghosting the cheap fiberglass sign. It was completely unmarked. From the outside it looked like the home of a hoarding madman. The two small front windows were blocked by piles of disorganized odds and ends, all of it for sale. She smiled when she thought of how Jiri could eyeball anything in the store and instantly bark the price to a shell-shocked customer. She crept up to one of the windows and peered between a small gap in the merchandise. The overhead light was off, but the store was always bathed in the pinprick sparkle of tiny red and green LEDs.

Then another light clicked on—a small flashlight—and floated around the middle of the room. The beam played along the piles of laptop computers, air conditioners, console games. The lonely Cabbage Patch doll. Mistletoe ducked out of the way as the beam swept across the window gap.

It won't end, she thought. *Ivor was right about Martin Truax: he will never rest.*

She slid the stunner out of her sleeve and crouched in the doorway to wait.

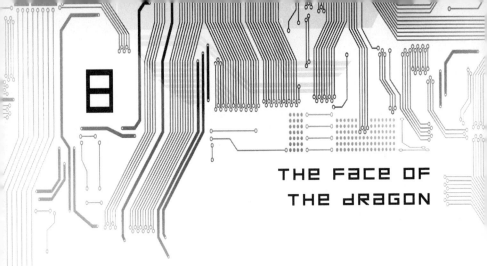

THE FACE OF
THE DRAGON

SONIA CARTER had big eyes full of glittering grays like the surface of a fast-moving river. They gave Ambrose the queasy sensation that Unison had inverted around him and formed a tunnel into her head. She accepted his Friend request. Her Thoughtstream blinked to life and meshed with his own.

Sonia Carter wonders why Takashi waits so long between visits.

Takashi Nakamura is 0111001101101111101110010011100 1001111001.

Binary, Ambrose thought. *He's excited.* They were standing in a small conference room—round table, a dozen chairs, no windows—deep within the labyrinthine guts of the Mass Entertainment Immersion Center, where Sonia had just finished giving a presentation to investors on the latest upgrade for her UniPetz Application. The upgrade allowed for the integration of a sentient pet into a user's Thoughtstream. Ambrose didn't really see the point of a window into the soul of a soulless creation, but figured it would be highly profitable.

All around them, ghostly investors chattered as they filed out.

Ambrose blinked away Sonia's hypnotic eyes. She wore a spotless white leather trench coat with a wide stripe of crimson near the bottom, where it enclosed a pair of black boots. A furry, ferretlike creature with a wrinkly nose curled around her ankle and busied itself with sniffing Takashi's Mood-shadow, which had reappeared as a pulsing red and orange splatter.

"Welcome to the MEIC," she said. Her voice was measured and restrained. *The opposite of Mistletoe's brash subcanopy patter,* he thought with a sharp and unexpected pang. He promised himself that he would shimmer out and check on her after he wrangled some information from Sonia, whose coolly professional gaze was making him uncomfortable.

"Thanks," he said.

"First time here, I take it?"

"Just created his Account today," Takashi said.

She smiled. "Shimmer-shocked?"

Ambrose played dumb. "I'm not sure."

"How's your throat feel? The residue builds up."

Ambrose gave her an exaggerated *gluuckkkk* and shrugged. "Fine, I guess."

Sonia waved to the last ghost, an old bald man, as he left the room. Ambrose and Takashi had missed the entire presentation, winding their way through the endless hallways of Unison's gaming epicenter. It had been a distracting journey. A user-created playground like the MEIC was something

Ambrose had no time for in his old life, so his awe at the sheer magnitude of the place was genuine. A peek inside one door revealed an infinite landscape of rolling hills, dense forests, and crumbling granite monuments to a civilization that had never existed: four-armed giants, their stone limbs stumped with age. Another door opened straight into the ocean. Ambrose had pressed his palm flat against the wall of water that rippled like a hanging sheet in the doorway.

"Let's walk," Sonia said as the plastic chairs in the conference room expanded, growing thick, cushiony arms and high-backed headrests. They looked like something out of an ancient Victorian drawing room. Ambrose shook his head in disgust, remembering that Adam Trevor was into furniture. Was Ivor determined to make this experience as irritating as possible?

The beige table became a deep, lacquered brown with dark grain patterns.

"Yes," Ambrose said, "Let's go somewhere else. Please."

Sonia and Takashi glanced at each other. Sonia's flat, businesslike expression softened. Ambrose felt a sudden burst of inexplicable closeness to her, as if they were old friends having a surprise reunion that required a long, warmth-sharing hug. Takashi's Thoughtstream was having a powerful effect on his own. Ambrose caught a fleeting impression of a moment he'd never shared with Sonia—some kind of gentle, dignity-preserving rejection—that made his throat constrict and his heart beat faster.

Takashi's crush on Sonia was so obvious it was embarrassing.

She opened the door, which had changed to a thick,

medieval-looking thing made of oak and held together with dark metal strips and huge black nails.

This is an exact replica of the door to King Richard III's throne room!

6,897 other users like this door.

Outside the conference room, the hallway was lined with bubbly temperfoam chairs, popular twenty years ago. Ambrose ignored the detailed furniture wikis instantly accessed by his Feed. He didn't care that temperfoam had its origins in the innovative mattress designs of the twenty-second century. For New User Adam Trevor, the MEIC was becoming a furniture museum.

Thanks, Ivor.

Ambrose wondered if Mistletoe was giving the old man a hard time. He hoped so.

"Geez," Takashi said, recoiling.

"Why does this place make you so angry, Adam?" Sonia asked.

His Thoughtstream was displaying his contempt. He shrugged. "Just thinking about something else."

"One thing you'll learn very soon is that fleshbound troubles cease to matter in here," she said.

"But not really—I mean, your problems out there don't just *disappear.*"

She nodded, accepting that he thought this to be true. They turned a corner and edged past a crowd of ghosts gathered around a Tetra Jack table. Metallic cards flashed over their heads and descended in a waterfall, reminding Ambrose of the monthly game he used to play with Len and some Programming Associates before they kicked him out for winning too often. His Process Flow ability, in addition to being the crux of the spooky genius that had defined his corporate identity, also made him a frustrating Tetra Jack opponent. And now that ability was gone. He could feel its absence in his mind, throbbing like an amputee's phantom limb. What if the procedure had extinguished it forever?

As they left the gamblers behind, Ambrose got a vague impression of their combined Thoughtstreams and winced at the seedy desperation.

"Junkies," Takashi mumbled.

"We all have our addictions," Sonia said. "You play Saturnine War RPGs; other people play Tetra Jack."

Ambrose glanced sideways at Sonia, suspicious of her lofty, maternal tone. She sounded more like one of his older friends than Takashi or Mistletoe. He wondered who the Sonia Carter Profile was hiding, and if his mask was as obvious as hers.

Maybe he was just being paranoid.

They turned another corner into the hallway of a cheap motel, all floral patterns and peeling wallpaper. Sonia's UniPet nuzzled his ankles.

"Friendly little guy," he said.

"Girl. And someday soon, we could all be like her."

"Girls?"

"No. Existing solely within Unison."

On the other side of Sonia, Takashi struggled to hold back

a proud grin. His Mood-shadow flared brightly. He'd taken Ambrose to the right Friend, and he knew it.

"You mean, like . . . permanent insertion?" Ambrose asked.

She glanced at Takashi, who shrugged.

"I've heard of it," Ambrose said quickly. "Everybody talks about it."

"Uh-huh," she said. "Listen, Adam, why are you here?"

"Takashi didn't . . . I guess I'm just curious, and Takashi figured you'd be able to help me out."

"But what I'm asking is, why did you create an Account in the first place?"

"We just got the money. My dad got a new job, and so for my birthday—"

"That's *how* you're here. I'm asking *why.*"

Ambrose was momentarily speechless. He hadn't expected her to interrogate him. Now he was sure that Sonia was a mask for an older user. Finally he said, "Because everybody else is already here. I felt like the last person in Eastern Seaboard City without a login, you know?"

He could tell by the coldness that crept into her Thought-stream—a tangible chill that scraped behind his eyes—that she was disappointed with his answer. He would have to be more specific if he hoped to learn anything useful. Playing detective from the bottom rung of Unison—no Admin Deck, no access, no network of Friends—was as foreign to Ambrose as the topside world would be to Mistletoe. He felt at odds with his useless furniture and apple-loving ID, and fought the urge to shimmer out.

"Sorry," he said. "I've just never thought about it before.

What I mean is, Unison seemed like . . ." He followed Sonia and Takashi through a door that led them out into the upper deck of an ancient Roman stadium. The hard granite benches overlooked an oval playing field of tightly packed dirt. The whole place was deserted. They sat. She looked at him expectantly.

He continued. "It seemed like something important was passing me by, and if I waited too much longer to join, it would be different . . . like, so far *beyond* me that I'd never be able to catch up. I mean, I heard they've already had one pretty serious upgrade, right?"

He congratulated himself on this conversational bait. Freelancers like Sonia were plugged into the Unison rumor mill. If his father had been operating outside the boundaries of UniCorp, hiding his personal project from Ambrose and the other Associates, Sonia might have picked up a stray piece of relevant cross-chatter. He watched as she slipped her right foot free of its boot and drew a line in the dirt with her big toe. A lion appeared at the edge of the field below and strolled lazily out to the middle, where it collapsed onto its haunches and rested its massive head on its front paws.

Takashi leaned forward and traced a parallel line with his finger. A fat red dragon with scaly wings folded back along its midsection slithered out from the other end of the field. The lion picked up its head and eyed the dragon warily.

"Well." Sonia turned to Ambrose. "For me it was mostly business. Where else can a fifteen-year-old girl make this kind of money? Out there, you need patents and teams of engineers. In here, you just need the raw material, the ideas and concepts."

If you're fifteen, I'm Adam Trevor.

"You don't program Apps all by yourself, though, right?"

"I'm a UniCorp subcontractor. They do the legwork and take a cut."

Ambrose was surprised at her candor. "So you're not really an independent developer?"

"As much as anyone is, I guess. If you think UniCorp doesn't have a hand in what you create in here, you're a fool."

"Like the MEIC," Takashi said. "It's a user-created and -maintained space, but UniCorp could pull the plug anytime they want. All this"—he gestured toward the lion and the dragon, which began circling each other carefully—"vapored away in a microsecond."

"Why would they do that?" Ambrose asked.

"Who knows what's going through his head?" Takashi said.

Sonia shot him a withering glance. Takashi's Mood-shadow diminished beneath the bench. He focused his attention on the field below, where the dragon had spread a pair of massive, translucent wings, inscribed with veins like bloodshot eyes. They flapped lightly, just enough to raise the dragon's body above the lion while keeping its tail on the ground. The lion pawed the dirt.

"Going through whose head?" Ambrose asked—but he knew.

Sonia bit her lip and gave Takashi a small nod. He grinned, and Ambrose felt a fierce upsurge in Takashi's Thoughtstream.

Takashi Nakamura wants lion blood.

The dragon folded its wings and dove straight for the lion's neck. The lion twisted sideways and the dragon sunk its dagger-teeth into the lion's furry back. The lion roared and was joined by a chorus of answering howls. Dozens of lions sprang from hidden pits and converged onto the dragon, which flapped madly upward, its long red tail flailing at snapping jaws. The dragon shrieked, and its own reinforcements swooped over the crumbling stone wall of the stadium in a scaly blur of red, yellow, and green.

Ambrose recognized the scheme: they were orchestrating chaos to cover a risky in-Unison conversation. A battle like the one raging around them could scramble UniCorp scans for a few precious minutes.

"Martin Truax," Sonia said, finally. "The creator. He who giveth and taketh away."

"What about him?"

"Chatter among freelancers like me is mostly speculation. Half of it's idle, half of it's strategic, designed to throw everybody off, make room for your own ideas, beat other homebrew types to the punch. But lately it's been off-the-charts twitter-brained. Like, Martin's gone rogue and even his own advisers don't know what he's up to, because he's planning to spring Version 3.0 on everybody unannounced, wipe everything that came before. Logins reset across the board. Profiles erased. People are saying there won't be any warning. No ramp-up. Just *zap*—he unveils the upgrade, and in the end nobody even *cares* that it's this big ambush because the opportunities are unimaginably game changing."

"Unison 3.0 will be, like, Humanity 2.0," Takashi said sagely, repeating some overheard catchphrase. "Might wanna duck. . . ."

Ambrose and Sonia leaned sideways as a yellow dragon tail whipped past and disappeared behind the upper wall. A whiff of acrid smoke lingered.

"So what's the big game changer?" Ambrose asked. "What's its function?"

Sonia herded her UniPet away from Takashi's Mood-shadow and plopped the squirming ball of fur into her lap. "My favorite theory? Unison's on its way to becoming the very first inter-dimensional travel agency. Shimmer in somewhere in ESC, shimmer out in the London Expansion, some off-world Saturnine base . . . or maybe to other places that aren't exactly on the map."

"Like where?"

"Who knows? Like I said, these are the rumors."

"And Marty's not giving a press conference anytime soon," Takashi said.

For the first time in his life, Ambrose considered the man he used to know as his father from an outsider's perspective. Martin Truax seemed as remote and impenetrable as the ivy-choked walls of his Unison estate.

"I guess we can't just ring the bell at Greymatter," Ambrose said.

Sonia's Thoughtstream cooled again. "You're the first new user I ever met who knew the name of the creator's estate."

Her UniPet stared at him with slit-eyed suspicion. Down on the field, the lions slunk away, licking their wounds. The drag-ons soared above in V formation and disappeared over the edge of the stadium. He'd made Sonia uneasy, and she was done talking to him.

"What about a time line on this upgrade? Any chatter about that?"

"Well," she said distantly as she stood up, "funny you should ask."

"Why's that?"

"Because some people I trust happen to think the gears are already turning."

"So when do these people think it started?"

"Yesterday."

She spun on her heel. He followed her toward a door marked EXIT in the boxy pre-Unison fashion. She stopped and turned, hesitating. Ambrose could practically *see* her train of thought: *should I let him know that I know he's after something bigger, or should I simply let it drop?*

She said, "You should be more careful. You don't know who you're dealing with."

Ambrose blinked in surprise. As she was speaking, a gold UniCorp *U* had appeared on the lapel of her jacket. He blinked again, and it disappeared.

From behind him Takashi said, "Hey, Adam."

Ambrose turned. His First Friend's straight black hair had been replaced by Martin Truax's unkempt sandy waves. Takashi stepped back.

"Adam, what's wrong?"

Now Takashi's mouth had become Martin's, too: the movie-star grin and brilliant white teeth. Ambrose felt a hand on his shoulder, glanced down at the *U* emblazoned on the gold cuff link, and spun, terrified.

Sonia was wearing his father's suit.

He fought a paralyzing wave of nausea that began in his stomach and shot through his limbs.

"This is bad," Sonia said, backing away. "This is all wrong."

Ambrose sank to his knees. The stone floor of the stadium felt spongy and elastic.

"Sonia?" Takashi squeaked.

Sonia's steel gray eyes narrowed in anger. Martin Truax's features struggled to eclipse her own: tan skin with a hint of manicured stubble rippling over her pale, smooth face.

"Adam?" Her voice was Martin's authoritative bark. "Tell me what you see!"

He looked away as Martin's broad shoulders filled out the suit. Ambrose tried to crawl, but his hands were too heavy to move. He looked down and screamed: they were pinned to the dirt with oversized *U* cuff links, golden spikes stuck right through his palms.

Somewhere far away Sonia screamed, "Shimmer out, Takashi!"

He felt their abrupt exit as a tiny scraping in his nasal passage.

Sonia Carter is currently fleshbound.

Takashi Nakamura is currently fleshbound.

Ambrose was alone. His hands were suddenly free. He scrambled to his feet. One of Takashi's green dragons was sitting on the granite bench, wings folded carefully against its scale-covered sides.

Ambrose backed away. His brain was throbbing, his vision shaky. His Profile felt distant and unimportant, a hazy memory.

"Oh, no . . ."

The dragon's elongated lizard head was topped with the sandy waves of his father's hair. It turned to him and grinned, revealing row upon row of perfectly modified white teeth. Pinned to the tip of each wing, a *U* cuff link sparkled.

When the dragon spoke, it sounded like his father's voice overlapping a thousand times.

"Daddy's very upset with you, Ambrose."

He slapped his palms together and shimmered out.

The Roman stadium receded as if it had been a picture dangled in front of his face and abruptly snatched away. The mirror that split his mind between real-time perceptions and his Profile shattered, leaving a second of frantic confusion in its place. Then he understood that he was Ambrose Truax, that he was encased in a hollow trunk of wires far beneath the streets of subcanopy ESC, and that he was in agonizing pain.

He blinked the world back.

His wounded palms sent stinging hot tracers up his arms.

Externalized data streams spiraled around him. He heard the heavy, rasping gulps of a person desperate for air and then realized that person was himself. His hands were paralyzed, suspended at his sides. He had a stomach-churning flashback to the Unison cuff links. What had just happened? His father had been everywhere and nowhere, all at once.

Not his father, he reminded himself. Not anymore.

"Get me out!" he called. He heard footsteps shuffling closer. They sounded lopsided, like one leg was heavily favored. Did one of the brothers have a limp? The wires of the trunk parted. Ivor poked his head inside and flashed that infuriating thin-lipped smile.

"Productive visit, I hope."

"Let me out."

The old man stooped to enter the enclosed space, then rose to his full height to disengage Ambrose's palms from the signal core.

"This might tingle."

Ambrose clenched his teeth as Ivor slid a long wire out from under the bandage on his right hand, then his left. Tears flooded his eyes. Ivor unwrapped each tender palm and slapped on a cool, foul-smelling muck before wrapping them with fresh bandages. The pain faded to a dull ache. Ambrose wiggled his fingers. Ivor turned and left the wire trunk without a word. Ambrose followed him.

The first thing he noticed was that the lab stank. After the carefully calibrated series of smells he'd experienced in Unison, the underground tunnel smelled wet—earthy and a little sour. The second thing he noticed was Ivor's pronounced limp, which was definitely new.

"What happened? Where's Mistletoe?" He looked around—no girl, no scoot. "And where's your brother?"

Ivor sank into a battered green armchair that he'd pulled in front of the pre-Unison keyboards. The goat-dog trotted over and curled up at his feet, horned head resting on furry paws.

"How was your preliminary investigation?" Ivor asked.

"Something happened in there. . . . I can't describe it. My father was everywhere, or pieces of him were. It was like he was part of the infrastructure, part of the *fabric*, which is impossible, I know. But . . . I've never seen anything like it."

Daddy's very upset with you, Ambrose.

He shuddered. Ivor said "Hmm," as if Ambrose had just described a particularly fine lunch he'd had. Something was wrong in this place, too. He turned to look at the front of the lab, the stacks of pre-Unison machinery, the iron door at the far end. The scoot was definitely gone.

He turned to face Ivor, half expecting his white hair to have turned sandy, his bulbous, misshapen nose to have become a perfectly sculpted triangle. But Ivor was still Ivor. Ambrose watched as he rubbed his shin through the folds of his gray robe.

"What happened to your leg?"

The goat-dog whimpered. Ivor winced. "An accident, while you were away."

Suddenly, Ambrose felt a simultaneous twinge of closeness and repulsion. It was a familiar feeling from his childhood, a deeply conflicted emotion that he'd never been fully able to understand. But it meant only one thing: his brother was nearby. He could practically smell the extrastrength BetterMint.

Ambrose stepped toward the old man. "What did you *do,* you lying—"

"It's not his fault, little brother." Len appeared in an open doorway to the right, next to an upended, dissected gasoline car. He stepped into the lab, flanked by eight burly Security Associates in black UniCorp jackets, stunners at their hips, assault disruptors slung across their backs.

Len's eyes flicked to his brother's bandaged hands and back up to his face.

"It's time to come home."

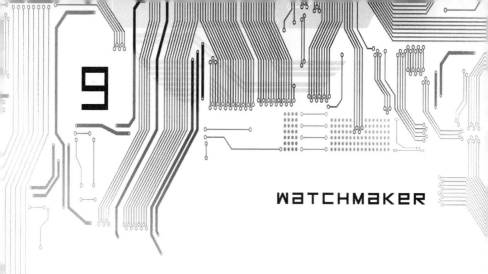

"**MISTLETOE!**"

Ma buh! She slunk farther into the shadowy doorway of Jiri's junk shop. Of all the moments to be recognized by one of her stupid neighbors, this had to be the worst.

"Hey, Mistletoe!"

The fat little boy was called Shampoo because of the noise he made when he sneezed. Eight or nine years old, he didn't seem to have parents. He was allergic to pretty much every-thing, and his face was covered in curious Dalmation smudges of permanent dirt. Sometimes Mistletoe slipped him leftovers from Dita's house.

She watched the boy waddle through subcanopy foot traf-fic. She couldn't let him corner her in the doorway—whoever was inside could open the door at any moment—so she eased along the front of the shop beneath the cluttered window. A quick glance inside revealed the bouncing flashlight beam. She wondered if the burglar had heard Shampoo yelling her name.

Beside her, the little boy puffed to a stop. He smelled like overripe fruit. A thick trail of snot hung from his nose.

"Hey, Mistletoe, where you been?"

"Come on," she said, grabbing the soft flesh of his upper arm.

"Ow! What're you doing—that *hurts*!"

She marched him around the corner and stopped behind a surprisingly green and healthy row of bushes. She pocketed the stunner and held him against the wall.

"W-what—"

"Listen to me, Shampoo. You didn't see me here. You don't know what happened to me, but I'm not around anymore. I left Little Saigon for good. Nobody knows where I went. Got it? Nod one time if you think you got it."

His eyes filled with tears. Mistletoe thought of the little bird that had fallen in front of her scoot. How tiny and delicate.

"Just friending *nod,* Shampoo."

He nodded frantically. Tears ran down his face, snaking pale, clean lines through the dirt. She let him go. He wiped his face with the back of his hand, leaving a smeary mess.

"Here," she said. "Let me." She reached with the corner of her sleeve, but he ducked out of the way and ran into the crowded street. She fought the urge to chase him down and explain that right now was a dangerous time to be her friend. They were both better off if he was simply afraid of her without knowing why.

She turned the corner and flattened herself against the wall of the abandoned florist. The topside cop who'd chased them before—the one with the hat—was holding the door open for his partner, Red. She curled up into a ball. Just another subcanopy urchin, sleeping in the street.

She opened one eye and watched as the cops melted into the crowd. Shampoo might have saved her life: she hadn't counted on *two* people being inside, and if they'd opened the door to find her waiting, she'd have been overmatched, despite her weapon.

She imagined the little boy huddled in some alley, wondering why the girl who'd always been so kind to him had suddenly turned vicious. *Stay away from me*, she thought. *I'm not who you think I am.*

I'm not even who I thought I was.

When the cops had been out of sight for a few minutes, she sat up and scanned the crowd. No familiar faces. At the door of the junk shop, she tried the handle. Hat and Red had locked it behind them. Next to the door was a square panel, slightly darker than the rest of the wall. She slid it aside. A keypad blinked to life. She entered Jiri's password, then placed her thumb against a small glass plate. Jiri may have been a lonely, secretive man, but he trusted her with his shop.

The door clicked and she slipped inside, where she promptly froze and waited for the horrible skittering to stop. The place was infested with cockroaches that scattered in every direction whenever a human interrupted their party. She hoped they'd freaked out the cops, at least.

When the store grew silent again, she moved quickly down an aisle of toaster ovens, past a bin of cell phones, to a closet at the back of the store. Here she slid aside a second keypad. Jiri had absolutely *not* trusted her with his special inventory, but she'd snooped and discovered his password. She waited for the click and pulled open the heavy door with two hands.

A dim light in the back of the long closet illuminated two neat shelves of metal weapons: short, nondescript stunner batons like the one she'd snagged from Ivor; long, hollow disruptors that fit over your forearm and tapered to a point when you made a fist; L-shaped handguns with pre-Unison parts. She scanned the row of disruptors until she found the smallest. Its gray casing was crisscrossed with deep scratches, revealing the silver plating beneath.

You match Nelson, she thought, slipping her hand inside until the tube covered her forearm. She closed her fist, and the orange point sprang forward into firing position in front of her knuckles. She flicked open her hand, and the point slid back into its casing, hiding the entire weapon beneath her sleeve.

"You need a name," she whispered. But nothing came to her.

Next to the shelves Jiri had stacked dusty boxes of bullets. She was working her way down the row of ancient ammunition when her shoe sent a metal object sliding across the floor. It hit the wall with an alarming *clank*. Cockroaches rearranged. She knelt and found a rectangular metal box the size and weight of the tattered dictionary Jiri had kept in the house. She shook it. The contents shifted with a feathery shuffle. She turned the box over in her hands but couldn't find the locking mechanism in the dim light. And there were no seams in the metal—the box was welded shut. What had been so important to Jiri that he'd locked it away inside the weapons closet?

With the disruptor beneath her sleeve and the box in her hand, she left the closet, pushed the heavy door shut, and waited for the cockroaches to reposition themselves in the dark. Then she crept down the aisle, past the massage chair Jiri never let anyone buy because she loved it so much. At the door she took one last look at the shop, then opened it a crack to peer out at the street. No sign of the cops. They could be watching somewhere, unseen, but that was a chance she'd have to take for the rest of her life. She stepped outside and shut the door behind her.

Back in the dim space beneath the porch where she had left Nelson, Mistletoe ran a finger around every inch of the box, feeling for the tiniest imperfection in the metal casing. Nothing. There was only one thing to do. She clenched her fist, and the disruptor sprang from her sleeve, closing around her hand. She flicked aside the safety lock with her thumb. Vibrations jiggled her arm and numbed the back of her neck. She shrugged away the strange sensation and placed her thumb against the bottom of the slide panel—the lowest power level, barely a spark—and the vibrations faded to a distant quiver. She shut one eye, aimed at the box, and jerked her elbow back.

The space beneath the porch lit up like a topside morning. The box leapt into the air, slammed against the ceiling, and burst open, scattering bits of paper like leaves settling in the street outside Aunt Dita's house. Frantically, she gathered them as they fell. The few pages that hadn't been scorched from the shot were covered in Jiri's messy scrawl. She salvaged the legible ones and crawled on her belly toward the edge of the porch nearest the street, where light seeped in. The unburned top half of the first page she held said:

2230. Final preparations in place. Operation to proceed.
2300. We are only four for this rescue—J, P, D, D. Topside in one

hour. Reach hospital at 0200. Free subjects in lab at 0230. No shooting if surprise succeeds. If not maybe we die. No more preparing. Only doing. Carpe somnium.

Mistletoe thought: *J = Jiri. D = Dita.* And the rescue had to be her own. That meant these notes were fifteen years old, like her. But who were the others, P and the second D?

She flipped the page. Jiri's writing became even shakier.

0530. Status report:
P killed. Single shot to nervous system.
Female subject freed. Bad intelligence for male subject. In different hospital. Different lab. No way to know.

Mistletoe thought of the dream she shared with Ambrose. It was the second part that was uniquely hers: clutched to Jiri's heaving chest as he ran, shooting wildly, the wires snaking out of her head and falling about her shoulders.

Female subject freed.

So they'd really just burst in and grabbed her from some sterile UniCorp scan-tube. Her hands shook. Several pages crumbled into blackened flakes. She sifted through the remain-der: detailed sales charts, inventory slips, yellowed receipts. Lists of Western English words written in Aunt Dita's neat, careful hand. *Cat. Bird. Dog. Fish.* Next to each word was a simple line drawing of each animal. Dita's old language lesson charts.

Bad intelligence for male subject.

She thought of Ambrose trapped inside the wire trunk, his bloodied hands plugged into Unison. Maybe it had been a mistake to leave him. She wished he were here. Crushing the charred scraps to dust beneath her boots, she wondered if she should head back down to the brothers' lab. She dragged Nelson out from beneath the porch and was about to pop on her riding goggles when she saw it: a red pre-Unison wristwatch that had been blown clear of her hiding spot. She picked it up. Still warm. The band was twisted and burned. The square face was blank except for three black letters: SCU.

She turned it over in her hand. How did it tell time? Was it even supposed to tell time? Five tiny silver buttons lined the side. She pressed them all in turn. Nothing happened. The watch was her one solid clue, and she'd broken it before it could give up its secret. She tapped it against the panel that shielded her scoot's expertly rebuilt transmission.

"What do you think, Nelson?"

She ran a finger along the three little gears hanging from the necklace underneath her shirt. If Sliv could fix a topside scoot, surely he could handle a simple thing like a watch.

"Yes, *that* boy." She gave Nelson a kick. "I know. Shut up."

Half an hour later, she tore down the side of a stack into the heart of Rio II. Nelson rattled beneath her, protesting the reckless speed. She threaded her way to the front of a caravan of scoots all jockeying for position on the choked road. The lenses of her goggles collected a red and black spatter that she smeared away with her sleeve. Rio II had a gnat problem.

She sped down an alley that smelled like fish guts. When she emerged, the old Saturnine War Veterans Hospital squatted before her like a giant spider, each long hallway a leg that jutted out from the crumbling center dome. The crowd thinned out—even people who didn't believe in ghosts tended to give the abandoned hospital a wide berth. According to Sliv, it was the perfect crash pad.

A quick ride alongside one of the spider legs brought her to the spot where he'd surprised her with the necklace: an old access door in the ground, half off its hinges. Beneath the triangle-shaped hole, cement stairs faded into darkness.

She cut Nelson's engine. The relative silence—voices mishmashed into a faraway murmur, scoot engines a faded whine—reminded her of the A.I. junk-transport road. She hopped off the scoot and walked Nelson carefully down the stairs in front of her, using his headlight as a lamp. She felt the reassuring weight of the stunner inside her sleeve.

The tunnel was empty. It was also very clean, with none of the dirt and debris that gathered in every corner of subcanopy ESC. Just smooth, gray cement stretching on into oblivion. She leaned Nelson against the wall and waited. Her presence wouldn't go undetected for long.

A sound in the darkness in front of her. *Tap-tap. Tap-tap-tap.* She held her breath. She listened.

Again, closer. *Tap-tap-tap-tap.*

She half expected a blind man to emerge from the darkness and shuffle past, his cane testing the ground in front of his feet. Instead, a metallic insect the size of a small dog appeared at the edge of the headlight's glow. It had titanium pistons for legs, which slid back and forth at the knee joints. Its head was a camera lens connected via two wires to some kind of alkaline battery on its back. The lens swept Mistletoe from head to toe and back again. Three silver gears attached to the battery turned in time with the camera's movements.

Mistletoe waved.

"Hey, Sliv," she said. Her voice echoed in the tunnel. The insect seemed to stare at her face for a moment before skittering backward into the darkness.

Alone again, she clenched her fist and the tip of the disruptor slid out of her sleeve. The insect reappeared, accompanied by a round plastic disc on wheels that bumped into the wall, changed direction, hit the other wall, and finally came to rest at her feet. An ancient stereo speaker lashed to the top of the disc crackled to life. Three silver gears turned along its side.

"Didn't expect it to be you, Anna," the speaker said. She recognized Sliv's voice behind the static.

"It's Mistletoe."

"What is?"

"My name."

"I forgot. Pretty fancy arm cannon you got there. Been doing some shopping?"

"Something like that." She opened her fist and the weapon retracted. "Listen, Sliv, I need your help."

The speaker spit out a burst of white noise. She cringed.

"Can I come in so we can talk?"

More static. The insect and the speaker disc retreated into the darkness. She waited a few minutes for some kind of further instruction and had just begun to press on down the hallway when she heard the echo of footsteps approaching.

Sliv stepped into view. Mistletoe covered her mouth to keep from crying out. The flesh on his left arm was gone, exposing an inner clockwork of thin metal pistons like the camera-insect's legs. Instead of a hand, three gleaming silver gears slanted toward one another, creating a hollow point.

"Nice to see you, too," he said.

She realized her eyes were probably wide with shock.

"It's nothing new—I always wear long sleeves out there," he explained, nodding toward the entrance to the tunnel.

"But your hand . . ."

He indicated a series of oversized bullets dangling from his belt. He pulled one off and fitted it to the gears at the end of his arm. The domed casing slid back, and flesh-covered fingers bloomed out. He wiggled them.

"You made that?" she asked.

"Mm-hmm," he said. "Wasn't hard."

"Topside tech?"

He leaned against the wall and brushed the shaggy brown hair from his eyes, smoothing it back behind his ears. "Big time," he said. Mistletoe squinted at him. Was the headlight casting a shadow beneath his nose, or was Sliv trying to grow a mustache?

"This is all my original skin," he said, pointing at his face.

She looked away and thought of Ambrose in his business suit, his floppy blond hair and perfect teeth, and realized that she had just compared Sliv to him without even meaning to.

"Sorry," she said.

"Don't be."

She pulled the burned wristwatch from her pocket and handed it to Sliv. "Any idea what this is?"

He scrubbed away the blackened ash with the front of his shirt, revealing the rest of the label: ESCU. Then he loaded another dangling bullet onto his gear hand. A set of screwdrivers and miniature wrenches fanned out in place of fingers. He pried the cover off the square face. Mistletoe leaned forward, curious.

"You're blocking my light," he said without looking up. She

backed against the wall to wait while he attacked the insides of the watch with a tiny screwdriver. A few seconds later, he snapped the cover shut and pressed one of the silver buttons.

An explosion like a pre-Unison flashbulb set the tunnel ablaze with white light. A luminescent jumble of sparks blinked and froze in the air between them. Sliv shook the wristwatch and slapped it once against the cement wall. The sparks reshuffled into tiny blocks of white text on a light blue externalized page.

"ESCU is Eastern Seaboard City University," Sliv said, bathed in the pale blue glow. "And this thing's an old coursework database. Research junk and homework assignments and stuff like that. It's a few years old—they stopped using 'em when most of their students got hardcoded."

Mistletoe scanned the page. There was a heading at the top:

COURSE # E-56.8
NAVIGATING THE UNISON
FREELANCE MARKETPLACE
PROFESSOR DEIRDRE O'HANLON

Deirdre. The second *D* Jiri mentioned in his notes?

Mistletoe knew exactly one thing about Eastern Seaboard City University: it was located above the canopy.

"I need to get topside," she said.

The course data vanished. Sliv pulled a long strand of hair from behind his ear and began to roll it idly between his thumb and forefinger. "We got foraging planned for tomorrow night. You're welcome to come."

"Who's 'we'?"

"Me and my gang."

"You're not in a gang."

"Yeah, I am. We're called the"—he glanced at Nelson, then Mistletoe, then the ESCU course database—"Watchmakers."

"Great name."

"Thanks. It's new. Like yours."

"I need to go up *now*, though."

He fiddled with another strand of hair and eyed her curiously. "Okay, Anna Mistletoe."

"It's just Mistletoe."

"Two conditions. One: you tell me why you're in such a hurry to get topside. Two: whatever you have to do up there, you take me with you."

"One: I can't. Two: I also can't."

"Thought you'd say that. It's a guy, then?"

This caught her off guard. "What? No, it's not—*ma buh,* Sliv, this has nothing to do with . . ." She sighed. "It's not about a *guy.*" She thought for a moment, chewing her bottom lip. "Do you know where you come from?"

He crossed his arms over his chest. The gear hand rested comfortably in the crook of his elbow. His sleeveless black shirt exposed the tattoo of a melting clock on his right shoulder.

"Same place as you," he said. "Little Saigon."

"Uh-huh. And you know who your parents are?"

"Sort of."

She stared at him. He looked away.

"Okay," he said. "You're tracking down your people."

I'm tracking down myself, she thought—but said, "That good enough for you?"

"Yeah," he said, after a while. "That's good enough for me."

* * *

The entrance to the airlock at the edge of Rio II was strewn with crumpled cans, greasy blankets, and soiled clothes. No wonder this place had a gnat problem. Mistletoe rested a hand on Nelson's handlebar and listened to the familiar subcanopy sounds, isolating each specific curse, laugh, and engine roar in case it was the last time she ever heard it. She didn't know what scared her the most: flash-coolant or the chance that she'd never see these streets again. She thought of Ambrose, in the same situation, swapping his topside life for a subcanopy one.

"The scoot stays," Sliv said.

"I figured."

"Won't fit," he explained.

"I *said* I figured."

She let go of the handlebar, thinking of all the afternoons she'd spent tipping Nelson through the trapdoor of her balcony, tearing down the stack, bouncing into the streets. The day Jiri had brought him home, he'd been gleaming, despite the missing chunks of paint and tarnished chrome. She felt like she was ditching her best friend.

"We'll take care of it," he said.

"*Him*," she corrected. "And don't just rip him up for the parts, either."

"Watchmaker's honor."

"Wait! You know what? There's this street kid from Little Saigon—Shampoo. Ask around, you'll find him. Give him the scoot."

"Shampoo?"

"Tell him it's from Mistletoe. Or just give it to him. It doesn't matter."

Sliv studied her, then nodded.

They watched a group of topsiders in green ESC Council Engineer jackets mill about the entrance. The engineers finished their drinks and tossed the empty cans on the ground. Mistletoe narrowed her eyes.

"They think it's one giant trash can down here."

"Easy," Sliv whispered, his hand on her shoulder.

One of the men looked in their direction, eyed them warily for a moment, then joined his coworkers inside the airlock. The door lowered behind them. Through the plexi, Mistletoe could see the lift ascend until the glass became a solid plasteel tube that merged into the shanty-stack overhead. She followed its invisible progress up through the stack, craning her neck to see the canopy. Above that, the airlock opened into topside ESC.

"So how do I go up the lift without an ID?" she asked. If she set off the trap's invisible trip wires, flash-coolant would trigger an alarm in a guardhouse nearby; cops and technicians would converge on the scene in a few minutes. She'd witnessed it a dozen times from the street: airlock closed, frozen corpse extracted. Then, while a crowd of onlookers gathered, a decision would be made to display or destroy.

Sliv lifted his gear hand. "You don't, unless you want one of these."

"Don't tell me that."

"See, the Rio II airlock never used to work right. We could slip past the sensors, no problem. We got pretty comfortable."

"What happened?"

"They fixed it."

Sliv pulled a silver clamshell from his belt and attached it to the gears. Mistletoe followed him around the side of the airlock and gagged. They'd waded directly into a pile of black trash bags. Most were torn open, oozing congealed rivers of garbage. She tasted the humid, rotten stench deep within her throat.

"This is friending awful," she choked. "What are we doing here?"

Sliv used a real finger to flick one side of the clamshell. Three copper keys emerged from its mouth. He sifted through chest-high garbage until he seemed satisfied by something she couldn't see. Then he plunged his hand straight into one of the bags. Mistletoe held her nose. Three faint clicks, and he pulled open a door that had been completely hidden by the trash.

He gave a mock-serious bow. "Princess, your ladder awaits."

Her eyes shot thirty stories up the stack to the underside of the canopy.

"It's an old access shaft for airlock maintenance," he said. "Bit of a climb, but it's all we got. You sure you don't want company?"

For a moment, she wished Sliv *was* coming topside with her. It would be nice traveling with someone who knew the territory. But even beginning to explain the purpose of her journey seemed impossible.

I just found out I was created by UniCorp. My parents are a metal tube and a couple of weird old men. Not sure what the point of my life is. Hoping to find that out, actually.

"I gotta do it alone. But thanks."

She peered inside the narrow access shaft. Sure enough, corroded metal rungs stuck out of the cement wall.

"Listen," he said, eyeing the necklace that had worked its way out from beneath her shirt. "Don't forget me, okay?"

She tapped his gear hand. "I won't."

Inside the shaft, she stepped on the bottom rung and looked up. Not even a hint of light to mark the exit. She took a deep breath and began putting hand over hand, pulling herself up through absolute darkness. A moment later, Sliv called to her.

"Hey!"

"What?"

"Have fun at college."

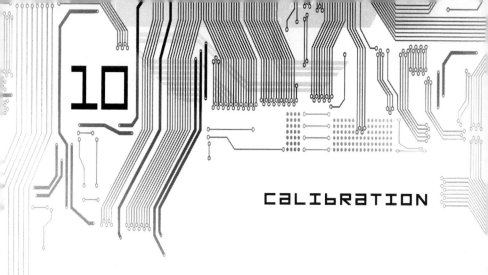

10

CALIBRATION

"**LEN,**" **AMBROSE** said, "you're a friending synth-toad."

He'd always had conflicted feelings about Len, but right now, miles beneath their childhood home and light-years away from their old life as UniCorp colleagues, Ambrose was pretty sure that he hated his brother. What did their shared childhood—the torment, mockery, and stray moments of surprising kindness—even mean anymore, now that he knew they weren't related?

"Impressive use of the local slang, little brother," Len said. "Might wanna put some more fierceness in the delivery, though."

"I'm not your brother."

"I know that. I just thought we'd ease into our new relationship."

Flanked by the unsmiling UniCorp security team, Len looked a bit like a young, earnest Martin Truax: the sandy hair and sharp features were the same, but the movie-star grin and magnetic presence were lacking. It seemed unlikely that Len was sent here to kill him—Martin would want his prize alive—but the standard-issue UniCorp disruptors had very effective nonlethal settings. If Ambrose tried to run, he'd be a quivering ball of floor jelly before he took three steps.

"How long have you known what I am?"

"About a year."

An absurd montage flashed in his mind: Len and Martin clinking wineglasses and howling with laughter at their shared joke, while Ambrose went blindly about his business like a rat in a maze.

He stepped forward. Eight Security Associates moved eight hands to eight stunners simultaneously. Ambrose displayed his empty, bandaged palms and turned to Ivor.

"What did he buy you with? A corner office at UniCorp? Full Admin access?"

The old man shook his head wearily and rubbed the scruff of his goat-dog's neck. "Len, please tell him the truth before he pinches a nerve in his face trying to give me a death stare."

Len gave a casual palms-down gesture to the security team. They took a step back and assumed at-ease slouches.

"Dita contacted me a year ago, Ambrose," Len said, switching to the warmer tone he used when giving presentations to UniCorp shareholders. "She hijacked my inbox, overrode my transfer log, same as you. *'Carpe somnium'* and all that. I dismissed it at first, but there was something about the initial message that kept me from bringing it straight to Dad."

Ambrose was stunned. "You're lying."

"Just listen. Partly it was his own behavior. You'd barely started working before his permanent insertion, so the man isolated in Greymatter is all you really know of his corporate persona. But I remember when he was still fleshbound, and it was a lot different. He's not himself anymore.

"The transmission inspired me to do some digging of my own. His private files don't exist, strictly speaking, so it was a challenge. And it was what I *didn't* gain access to that made me suspicious. Greymatter used to be transparent, or at least accessible to the highest-level Associates. We used to be allowed inside. Remember, we had Friday product meetings there for a while? Now it's a fortress. There's something there, something off-the-charts huge, and whatever it is, he's operating it outside the bounds of UniCorp. These guys"—he nodded at Ivor, who was giving his full attention to his shin—"at least offered the beginning of an explanation."

Ambrose considered the nineteen-year-old he'd always thought of as his obnoxious older brother. A world in which Len was his secret ally was hard to accept.

"So," Ambrose said. "You've known the truth about my . . ."

"Creation."

". . . for an entire year, and you never thought to mention it to me?"

The goat-dog barked happily.

Ivor said, "We realize now that it may have been a mistake to keep you in the dark."

Ambrose was incredulous. "Apology not accepted."

"We believed you were most effective as a deep-cover operative," Len said. "As soon as Dad revealed your purpose, we were going to have you extracted. Unfortunately, this meant cutting you out of the loop. And waiting."

"Come on, Len, deep-cover operative? You were using me,

just like Dad." He shook his head. "Just like *Martin.* You stood there and let me go through with the procedure."

"The one that you begged to undergo? We thought it would make you a more effective operative."

"Stop calling me that."

"These people"—Len gestured toward Ivor—"are not unlike UniCorp in that they're willing to take risks in the short term with the expectation of greater payoff. It was Dita who disagreed and slipped you the transmission without telling anyone. We were all taken by surprise. I had to send someone to intercept you."

"Jiri," Ambrose said, his mind racing alongside Len's explanation. He sent Dita a silent *thank-you* for being the one person who felt he deserved to know the truth.

"Which brings me to the fundamental problem with your frantic escape," Len said. "The calibration."

The word hit Ambrose like the shudder of anxiety that tightened his chest whenever he left a responsibility dangling for too long at work. In the rapid-fire chaos of the past two days (had it only been two days?), he'd forgotten about the second part of the procedure. The hypothalamus modification had been successful—he hadn't slept, wasn't tired—but the follow-up calibrations were necessary to prevent side effects. Without the release valve of dreaming, he would begin to process events like an insomniac. His subconscious would assert itself in his waking life. Eventually, it would fragment beyond repair and he'd be just like the early test subjects: a drooling, paranoid mess adrift in a world of hallucination.

He pictured Martin's leering face on the dragon's body.

It had already begun.

"Oh," he said, feeling very much like a scared, insecure younger brother.

"Right," Len said. "*Oh.* So we need to get back to the office."

"That's a poorly conceived plan."

"It's the only place that's equipped to handle the aftermath of a Level Seven. Come on, Ambrose, you know that."

"It just seems . . ." *Like a trick,* he thought. Like something Martin would do to get him to walk right back through the door of UniCorp HQ with minimal hassle. "Where's Mistletoe?" he asked Ivor.

"Your charming counterpart took off. Behold, her parting gift." The old man lifted up his robe to display an ugly bruise on his shin.

"I have to find her," Ambrose said. The thought of losing her forever made him feel deeply alone. She was the only other person who could understand what it felt like to find out you weren't quite human.

"First we have to get you calibrated," Len said. "The new ID Ivor hardcoded into you should work topside, so as long as we take my private entrance to the lab instead of walking in the front door—"

"I never knew there was a private entrance."

"There is. It's mine."

Ambrose still wanted to run. He wanted to find Mistletoe and escape Eastern Seaboard City together. But Len was right about the urgency of the calibration. He imagined a world filled with grinning Martin-dragons and shuddered.

"Fine," he said to Len. The security team stood at grim-faced attention. *Where do they find these guys?* Ambrose imagined a silent waiting room packed with beefy goons. "Let's get this over with."

They emerged from the subway tunnels into the streets of Little Saigon and jogged toward a long, black, cylindrical transport across the street. The security team lowered flaps on their windbreakers to cover the UniCorp insignias. The side of the transport said, in bright red letters, ENJOY RED SQUIRREL TEA. Beneath the letters was a picture of the green, black, and orange pellets available from Red Squirrel.

"Tea delivery?" Ambrose asked as they piled in. He noted a ninth member of the security team, who had been waiting in the control seat.

"I'm sorry for not getting your approval for the cover vehicle," Len said. "Short notice."

Len's voice could be like fingernails scraping plasteel. Ambrose winced. "Just making sure I wasn't seeing things."

"There's no one I can trust at UniCorp. I can't exactly requisition manpower and luxury transports to chauffeur you to HQ."

Ambrose glanced warily at the security team.

"They're my guys," Len said. "Report directly to me. Dad has no oversight."

"You think."

"I know. So what did you find out when you were logged in?"

The transport pulled out into traffic and promptly sat still. Then the lifts engaged and they glided over the tops of the stalled scoots and carts.

"I'm sure *that* won't draw attention to us," Ambrose said, mimicking Len's voice.

"If you'd rather we sit in subcanopy gridlock, I can tell the driver to put her back down."

Ambrose sighed. "Okay. First thing. Can you give me back my Admin Deck?"

Len shook his head. "Maybe I can restore some backend privileges while you're being calibrated, but I can't give you Admin. They'll trace a new high-level presence exactly one second after you shimmer in."

"Then what am I supposed to do? Admire the furniture? I'm supposed to be finding out why I exist."

"What did you find out?" Len prompted again. Ambrose wondered if his brother was being pushy because Martin was listening in. Then he remembered that paranoia was one of the side effects of the Level Seven.

"Who are these people you're working with, Len?"

"Actually, Dad's right about them: they're basically low-level saboteurs."

"Terrorists."

"Eh. They told me the truth. Dad stopped doing that a long time ago."

"What do they want?"

"Magnus and Ivor have been nursing a grudge against UniCorp ever since they got fired fifteen years ago. They had allies who either died or drifted away over the years. Finally possessing both you and the girl is a major victory."

"Nobody possesses me. And Mistletoe's gone."

"Good. We're all better off if she disappears. My priority is you."

"I'll go find her myself if I have to."

"You'll go where? Back to Little Saigon? Scream her name in the streets?"

Ambrose nodded. "If I have to."

"Don't be stupid."

"You don't get to tell me how to *be* anymore, Len."

The Security Associate sitting next to Len struggled to control his smirk. His mouth twitched and spasmed. Ambrose wished he could see what he looked like when he tried to be forceful and assertive. Apparently, it was hilarious. He wondered if his UniCorp colleagues had been laughing at him for years, if he'd been too blinded by his own last name to see the contempt all around him.

Paranoia.

Ambrose turned and shifted his attention to a scene out the window. The entrance to a topside airlock was swarming with subcanopy cops. They parted to clear the way for a pair of technicians in white thermal suits and helmets. Someone in the crowd tossed a banana peel that hit a cop in the shoulder and slid down his back. The other cops drew their stunners. Then the transport turned a corner and the scene disappeared behind a shanty-stack.

"Anyway, you know the Unison backend better than almost anyone," Len continued. "You should be able to translate your skill set into a query system to filter out the gossip and define the next steps in your investigation. If it were me, the first thing I'd do would be to—"

"Okay, Len, seriously, just shut up for one second. There was this freelance App creator who told me the cross-chatter about Greymatter's been freaky lately. Like, Martin's Version 3.0 might have already started. I asked her when the gears started turning, and she told me yesterday."

"See, now that makes sense—as soon as you ran, he had to act. You probably made *him* jump the gun, too. Which means he's doing two things at once: rushing to get his project off the ground and searching for you."

The transport merged onto the access road that encircled Rio II and cruised next to all manner of long, unwieldy commercial vessels heading for the topside dock. Ambrose watched as the transports in line ahead of them were boarded and searched by helmeted canopy cops on black scoots. When one of them pulled alongside the cover vehicle, the driver palmed down the window and said a few words to the cop, who saluted once and left them alone.

"Huh," Ambrose said. "Red Squirrel Tea."

Len gave a hearty thumbs-up. "People love it."

The interior of the transport lit up when they reached the surface as Len and the security team externalized their personal Inboxes. Ambrose unraveled his bandages and winced. One small, neat hole marked the center of each palm, where Ivor had rebooted his hardcoded ID. The wounds were still raw but no longer bloody. Ambrose had always healed quickly: scrapes and bruises often faded in less than a day. Vitamin-rich synth-food saw to that. Or maybe Martin and the lab Associates had simply *made* him that way? He wondered if he had vast reserves of untapped power. If regular human beings used only a fraction of their brain, how much of his was left to explore?

He flipped his palm and externalized the standard welcome page, something he hadn't seen in years. His heart sank as he realized that all of his settings had been wiped clean. Well, what did it matter? Ambrose Truax had been a sort of fake ID, too. *Mistletoe had the right idea*, he thought. *At least she'd chosen her own name.* He wondered where she was, and for a few seconds his mind drifted out over topside Eastern Seaboard City. He pictured her darting between atmoscrapers, snagging a BetterPear from a synth-cart, wandering shell-shocked into one of the vast indoor shimmerdomes, where people enjoyed their Unison experience from the comfort of recliners and beds, their motionless fleshbound bodies protected by guards who patrolled the mile-long aisles.

But that was all crazy; she couldn't even go topside. Wherever she was, he hoped she was safe. And as much as he wanted to find her, part of him knew that she was better off staying far away.

"We're here," Len said, tense and serious.

Ambrose vapored away the pleasant green welcome page. One of the Security Associates tossed him a clean piece of gauze, which he ripped in half and wrapped twice around each palm.

"I'll get you a new suit up in the lab," Len said.

Ambrose realized his skinsuit had been torn in several places, resulting in a faint, fragmented projection of the sharp blue holo-suit he'd worn to the procedure, a lifetime ago.

"I don't want to wear suits anymore," he decided suddenly.

Len sighed. "Fine, Ambrose, wear whatever you want."

Ambrose felt a queasy upsurge in his stomach. Len's face grew outward from his head and elongated to a point around the nose. His skin stretched to fit the inhuman skull shape. Long red welts appeared, like wounds from a medieval flogging. The welts oozed and broke apart to reveal a new skin of green scales. His eyes narrowed to yellow slits.

Ambrose screamed.

Len grinned, exposing Martin's impossibly white teeth. His grin widened. All Ambrose could see were rows upon rows of teeth, stretching back into oblivion. The gaping mouth blotted out the inside of the transport. A great wind howled in his ears, as if he were standing alone in the middle of an empty field. He felt—but could not see—a slimy tongue slither around his entire body. It began to squeeze the breath out of him, tighter and tighter, until a rib snapped like a twig. He tried to cry out in pain. The air stopped dead in his throat. It felt as if he were being held underwater. Then it was over.

He opened his eyes, even though he didn't remember having closed them.

He was sitting across from his brother in the transport. His heart was pounding.

Len was staring at him critically, one eye squinting more than the other. He didn't look shocked or disturbed. The security team filed past them, out of the parked transport.

"Is this the first incident?" Len asked.

Ambrose blinked away the afterimage of the dragon's face, burned into his memory like the outline of a bright light. The fear hit him all at once: *I am going insane.* He took a deep breath and gingerly pressed a finger into his ribs. No pain.

"Let's just do this."

He climbed out of the vehicle into a dim, windowless dock that smelled moist and subterranean.

"We're inside the canopy itself," Len explained. "Part of the old network of research and development labs directly beneath the UniCorp building." He palmed a spot in the blank gray wall, and a hidden door slid open. Ambrose followed his brother into a surprisingly plush elevator, like the one in the lobby.

The security team crowded in around them. Ambrose felt the butt of a disruptor press into his back.

"Sorry," mumbled one of the Associates—the first time Ambrose had heard any of them speak.

As the elevator sped silently upward, Ambrose attempted a quick Process Flow. His ability churned, running on fumes, making him dizzy. He thought he sensed a shadowy progression of events like forgotten words on the tip of his tongue. A single murky endpoint emerged: his likelihood of finding Mistletoe increased in Unison.

That didn't make any sense. She didn't even have a login ID. His ability was still haywire.

"Floor three seventy-five," Len announced. The Security Associates made a few imperceptible shifts in weight. Two or three cleared their throats.

Ambrose had a sudden memory of an American History wiki he'd studied years ago: skinny, grim-faced soldiers not much older than Len, huddled together aboard a primitive steel box of a boat, waiting for the ramp to fall open onto the beaches of France. And then he remembered the next image in the series, the tightly packed pile of motionless bodies that had moments before been young men.

"Wait," he said to Len, but it was too late. The door slid open.

The lab was dimly lit and empty. Ambrose exhaled. Len gave him a concerned look as the security team stepped into the room and began an efficient sweep, disruptors extended. Eventually one of the Associates beckoned with a quick wave.

"Clear," Len said, and stepped out. Ambrose followed. The door slid closed behind them and disappeared into the wall. They were behind the scan-tube platform. Ambrose walked up the steps and ran his hand along the smooth, cool steel of the closed tube, the instrument that had changed his life forever.

Carpe somnium, Ambrose.

Coming back to UniCorp HQ reminded him of everything he'd given up. What if he'd chosen to ignore Dita's transmission?

"Give me a hand with this, Ambrose," Len said, waving him down off the platform. But Ambrose lingered with the scan-tube, the machine as much a father to him as Martin Truax. He remembered the Friday product meetings in Greymatter. Concerning his company and its social network, Martin's awareness was absolute, down to the smallest detail. It didn't make sense for Len and Ambrose to have made it this far undetected. Ambrose looked around the darkened lab at the scan-tubes that crouched in the shadows. Something vague and unpleasant was nagging at him.

"Len?"

Len was busy externalizing a colorful lineup of charts, brain scans, and Process Flow documentation.

"Hmm?"

"Something's wrong."

"Give me a minute."

"No," Ambrose said, stepping off the platform and into the path of a rotating brain stem.

"Get out of your head. I'm trying to work."

"This is too easy."

Len pushed him aside.

He's troubled by it, too, Ambrose thought. Then he had the dreamy, time-slowing feeling he'd had on Dita's street, just before her house exploded. He remembered the leaves falling faintly through the air, the last one touching the ground right before—

"Run," Ambrose said.

"*I'm afraid I can't let you do that,*" a voice whispered in his ear.

"He's here!" Ambrose screamed.

Len narrowed his eyes. "Get in the scan-tube."

"I'm not crazy, Len. It's Dad!"

Len waved over two Security Associates. "Get him in the tube."

Instead, one of the Associates tossed Len a spare disruptor and pointed to the door of the lab as it slid open. Len struggled to attach the oversized weapon. His fist trembled.

"*Welcome home, Ambrose,*" the voice whispered.

UniCorp Security Associates—real ones—poured into the room through the open door, a phalanx of heavy boot steps and bristling disruptors. Len's Red Squirrel Tea unit took cover, crouching behind the row of smaller tubes in front of the platform. Len yanked Ambrose down.

"You brought me back to him," Ambrose said, feeling like a fool who had learned too late not to trust *anyone*.

Len clasped Ambrose's sore hand. "I won't let him take you, little brother."

Martin's voice boomed. "To the Security Associates currently protecting my sons: the first one of you to turn them over to my men will be rich. The rest will die."

"Get in there." Len pointed urgently at a tube halfway down the row. "It's an exit, Ambrose—*trust me.*"

Ambrose hesitated. Trust had gotten him trapped here, in the room where it had all started, at the mercy of the man who created him.

"Version 3.0, whatever it is—throw yourself into the gears. Don't let him upgrade." Len finally managed to slap his disruptor into place. Then he gave a low, sweeping hand signal to the men hiding alongside him. Each man gave a quick nod in return.

"Go now!" Len commanded as he and his men flipped their palms. An externalized UV shield appeared as a floor-to-ceiling wall of white light. Ambrose squinted at the barely tolerable brightness. The other side, he knew, was as blinding as an unblocked sun.

The static crackle of disruptor fire bounced around the lab. The Red Squirrel Tea Associate next to him screamed, his body jerking and convulsing in midair, suspended by the pulse that enveloped him. His arms bent back at an impossible angle before the pulse threw him to the floor.

The UV shield was distracting but as penetrable as smoke.

With a rough parting shove from Len, Ambrose moved toward the exit tube in an awkward crouch. The Red Squirrel team returned fire, their disruptors filling the room with fully automatic *thwunk-thwunk-thwunk* sounds.

His father's voice was audible above the cacophony. "Leave the younger one alive." And at the same time, it whispered into his ear, "*You won't be harmed, Ambrose. You're part of me. Part of Unison.*"

When Ambrose reached the exit tube, he glanced back at Len, who was firing madly through the externalized shield, oblivious to the return pulses blazing past his head.

Ambrose knelt and raised the lid of the tube. A UniCorp

Associate barreled through the wall of light—a momentary silhouette—and leapt at the Red Squirrel man next to Ambrose. They collapsed in a heap. A long knife flashed.

Ambrose scrambled up into the tube, keeping the lid between himself and the UniCorp barrage. As he pulled it shut, he saw Len's shoulder catch a green pulse that spun him around. An orange burst struck his neck and tightened like a glowing noose. Len clutched at his throat and sank to his knees.

As time seemed to slow once again, Ambrose thought of the marble he'd tossed off the edge of the Gen-Farm to impress his brother so many years ago. He saw it now, spinning for an endless millisecond in the empty air between atmo-scrapers, before it fell straight and fast through the clouds and out of sight.

He'd give anything to go back to that day, to run laughing after Len as they raced across the field past cloned cattle and synthetic goats.

As the lid shut, the noise of the battle receded. Beneath him, the metal tube sloped downward and formed a small tunnel. His brother was right: this was the only way out.

As always, Len was one step ahead.

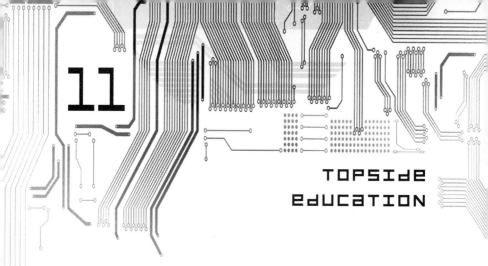

11

TOPSIDE EDUCATION

NIGHTTIME IN Eastern Seaboard City. Mistletoe stood at the edge of a four-lane street. The articulated frame cars passed in the perfect, never-ending procession she knew from all those afternoons staring up through the airholes. Their collective hum wasn't much louder than the distant rumble that filtered down through the canopy. She crossed her eyes slightly so that the single headlight on each car blurred into the one behind it and the lanes became unbroken lines of white light. All around her, atmoscrapers stretched up between the traffic streams like massive fingers poking through a glove.

She wished someone were here to share this sight with her, but even Nelson was gone. She felt incredibly alone, and not in the way she'd always craved. She longed for Ambrose's soft hand to hold. She imagined him standing next to her now, pulling her close among the dazzling patterns of light.

Across the street, the topside entrance to the airlock rose out of the ground, a sleek plexi cylinder capped by a round black roof with a green light poking up from the top. She guessed that was topside ESC's way of telling people that the airlock was in service. But what people? She looked back and forth. Endless cars. No pedestrians.

She walked up the deserted sidewalk to the first storefront, which turned out to be a series of silver boxes emerging from a gently glowing panel in the wall. Each box was emblazoned with a bold *U*. A sign floated above the boxes: ENJOY BETTER-FOOD!

Simply reading the word *food* sent sharp hunger pangs shooting across her midsection. She tried to remember how long it had been since she'd eaten anything. What kind of top-side cuisine was in these boxes? She peered above, below, and between each one, but there was no visible way to order food. And anyway, she didn't have any money. She didn't even have a hardcoded ID. She wondered if she would trip an alarm if she opened a box.

Her gnawing hunger urged her on.

She reached for the nearest box and froze. Someone was behind her.

"Psst! Kid!"

She turned. A yellow cab idled halfway up on the sidewalk. It was boxier than the teardrop-shaped cars that most topside people drove. There was a figure in the driver's seat, shrouded in shadow. She clenched her fist. The disruptor slid out of her sleeve.

"What do you want?"

Her voice sounded loud and harsh up here, with only the smooth traffic hum to compete with. She realized that she was still wearing her orange riding goggles around her neck and felt absurdly out of place.

"Need a lift?"

She stepped forward cautiously, disruptor raised. The driver had wispy black hair combed over to one side. He squinted through a pair of thick glasses perched at the tip of his nose. A pair of fuzzy holo-dice hung from the rearview mirror.

"You a long way from home, girl." He grinned, revealing a row of gold teeth.

She thumbed the panel on the side of the weapon. The tip glowed orange. Vibrations tingled her arm.

The cabbie displayed his empty hands. The sleeves of his neon blue shirt were decorated with tropical plants. "That how you treat a guy who offers you a ride?"

"It's how I treat everybody."

He pushed his glasses up to the bridge of his nose, then picked at the corner of his mouth. "Okay, then. Good luck."

Mistletoe thought quickly. This might be her best chance. "Wait." She moved her thumb away from the panel and disarmed the weapon.

He cocked his head politely.

"I just need directions. I don't have any money to pay for a ride."

He shifted in his seat, dislodging his glasses. "Where you tryin' to get?"

"ESC University."

He nodded thoughtfully. "That's pretty far."

"How long will it take me?"

"On foot? Two days."

Mistletoe's arms and legs were already sore from the climb up the access shaft. And she couldn't waste two whole days wandering the streets. She unclenched her fist and the disruptor slid out of sight.

"I have this," she said, reaching behind her neck to undo the clasp of her necklace. She held it up for him to see. The three silver gears spun in the air. She thought of Sliv standing among the putrid garbage at the bottom of the ladder.

The cabbie flashed his gold teeth. "That should cover the fare."

She hesitated. "If you try anything, I'll kill you. I won't even think about it first."

He nodded gravely. "Understood."

The back door swung open. Mistletoe slid into the leopard-spotted back seat. It smelled overly sweet, too much cheap air freshener. She pulled the door shut. The cabbie turned and extended his hand.

"Panda skin?"

He offered her a black-and-white-striped wafer that smelled like an onion. Mistletoe shrank back against the seat. She was starving, but the panda skin made her stomach turn.

"Can we just go?"

The cabdriver palmed a panel on his dashboard. The lifts engaged harder than Mistletoe thought possible for such an old car. They shot up over the ground-level traffic flow and skimmed along the top. The driver flipped the smelly wafer into his mouth and chewed with loud, happy smacks. Mistletoe wondered if she'd made a huge mistake by getting in this cab. Then she looked out the small window above her head and forgot everything except the new world outside.

The sky was as black as the access shaft. In Little Saigon, it was always a weak and sickly shade of day, depending on the quality of the lights hanging from the canopy. She had never lived in a place governed by the actual laws of dawn and dusk.

The cab careened around the edge of an atmoscraper. One traffic flow was briefly replaced by another before the world disappeared entirely.

"Where are you—" Mistletoe said, but the lights of the city returned as they shot out from under a short bridge. She slammed into the door as they spun around to join a single line of cars coasting up the side of a massive translucent dome lit from within by a soft yellow light.

"Shortcut," the cabbie said. As they crested the dome, she rose to her knees and peered out the side window. Looking down through layers of spotless plexi, she saw a vast honeycomb of white beds. Each bed contained a person sleeping with hands clasped together. Guards in UniCorp windbreakers patrolled the aisles. Little A.I. drones buzzed around the upper levels.

"What is this place?"

"Shimmerdome Nine. See, you pay for the privilege to occupy one of those comfy beds for as long as you want while you're in Unison. That way you're protected. No one comes and messes with you if you wanna stay inside for a few weeks."

"So all those people are logged in."

"Enjoying BetterLife as we speak."

They looked so peaceful. So different from Ambrose, stuck inside the wire tree trunk with all the raw externalized data racing around him. *Funny*, she thought. *I'm up in his world, and he's down in mine.*

They sped down the other side of the dome and joined the elevated traffic flow for a few blocks before diving to street level. Here, a few pedestrians loitered beneath a pyramid-shaped sign that proclaimed DRINK SPECIALS W/ STUDENT ID. The cabbie veered left and entered a narrow alley. They emerged into an enclosed field ringed with atmoscrapers and lit by millions of incandescent lights that hung in the air like tiny stars.

The cab stopped. They were surrounded by greenery—lush hedges and pine trees that dwarfed the anemic subcanopy shrubs. Here and there a stone roof poked above the foliage.

"Here we are, kid."

She looked out both windows. "Where?"

"ESCU."

"Looks like it hasn't been built yet."

He shrugged. "I didn't design the place, okay?" He rested his open hand on the seat divider and wiggled his fingers. She dropped the necklace into his palm, and he hung it from the rearview mirror.

The door clicked open, and she stepped out onto the spongy grass. The cab sped away into the night. She reached up and touched one of the low-hanging lights, a bright smudge in the night sky no bigger than her thumbnail. A faint chime rang. High above, another answered. She couldn't stop staring up. No canopy! Her heart pounded. Her stomach gnawed itself. Were any of these plants good to eat? She walked into the under-brush, hoping to find a path. As the hedges thickened around her and gnarled roots began to claw at her toes, she gave up walking and sat beneath a tree, pressing her back into the rough bark. She rocked back and forth slowly, listening to the soft chiming of the lights.

Soon she was lying down, eyes closed, breath steady. She was exhausted. The strange new world of light and speed withdrew to a distant point and disappeared.

Alone in a quiet forest in the middle of the busiest city in the world, Mistletoe slept.

Sometime later, a finger tapped her shoulder. *Wake up.* The tapping grew more insistent. *Wake up.* She sprang up against the tree, swinging the disruptor in a wild sideways arc as she blinked away sleep. Bright light filtered down through the tree-tops and swam in patches on the frightened girl who'd shaken her awake. She was older than Mistletoe, dressed in a long skirt that reminded her of Ambrose's suit, the way it fluttered in an unseen breeze and you could almost but not quite see through it. Slung around one shoulder was a beaded purse, more solid looking than the skirt. Her hands were raised high in the air.

"What do you want?" Mistletoe asked hoarsely.

"To see if you were okay. That's all. Swear on my ID."

Mistletoe realized how she must look in her dirty scoot-riding clothes and crusty blue pigtail. She straightened her posture and cleared her throat.

"I'm fine." She made a show of disarming and hiding the disruptor. "Sorry."

The girl dropped one arm and nervously twirled a strand of her long red hair with the other. "So, are you looking for the tour group, or . . ." She appraised Mistletoe from head to toe. "I have some food, if you're hungry."

Mistletoe wanted to scream *YES.* Instead she nodded warily. The girl opened the bag and hurriedly produced a foil-wrapped bar.

"It's not BetterFood," she said apologetically. "It's made from real milk, so it might taste a little weird."

Mistletoe's stomach was an instant black hole. Real milk chocolate was an expensive black-market commodity in Little Saigon, a once-a-year treat. She snatched the bar greedily and tore away the wrapper, barely noticing the tiny beam that sizzled from beneath a nearby bush, vaporizing the shiny foil before it could litter the ground.

The chocolate tasted rich and sweet and delicious. Just a hint of bitterness. She closed her eyes as she ate. Perfect.

"I also have some tea, if you're thirsty." The girl held out a small red pill.

Mistletoe wiped her mouth on the back of her hand. The instant rush of real sugar made her head swim. She eyed the pill. "No, thanks. I'm looking for Professor Deirdre O'Hanlon."

"Oh! I didn't realize you were a student. Did you check the directory?"

Mistletoe shrugged.

The girl looked confused. "Well, that's okay." She flipped her palm. A pale blue sphere appeared in the air between them, orbited by a thin planetary ring labeled ESCU DIRECTORY. Mistletoe blinked and tried to remain unimpressed, even though she'd never seen information externalized like this before. She remembered Ambrose trying in vain to get a signal below the canopy. Everyone up here probably did this palm flip a hundred times a day.

"Professor Deirdre O'Hanlon," the girl said. She poked the sphere with her finger, and it changed shape to become a three-dimensional image of a smiling woman about Aunt Dita's age. "Applied Unison Freelancing and Application Market Analysis. Is that her?"

"Um," Mistletoe said.

"She keeps a fleshbound office here on campus. If you're lucky, she'll have office hours today." The girl vapored away the directory and held out her hand. "If you authorize, I can transfer."

Mistletoe crossed her arms. "Transfer what?"

"The directions? To her office?"

"You can just tell me how to get there."

Fifteen minutes later, Mistletoe was standing next to a gray stone monument. It was a simple, unadorned cube, slightly taller than the trees and as wide as her subcanopy home. There were no doors or windows.

"Hello?" she called. At doorknob height in front of her, she noticed a handprint indented in the stone. She filled it with her hand. Nothing happened; she needed a hardcoded ID to proceed. She thought for a moment, then stepped back to mingle with the moving crowd on the path alongside the cube, strolling down and back without meeting the curious eyes of the holo-clothed students. She wondered if they were all rich like Ambrose.

When a boy with long dreadlocks tied back in a thick ponytail palmed open the cube, she rushed to squeeze in behind him.

Two steps through a narrow stone archway, she was shocked to find herself in the lobby of an enormous classroom building. The forest and surrounding atmoscrapers were gone. Gleaming walkways intersected above her head. A large glass box sat in the middle of the room, stuffed with armchairs and beds full of motionless students, hands clasped together. Others milled about the lobby and gathered around rows of silver boxes like the ones she'd seen last night.

Mistletoe crossed the lobby to a long row of blue doors: professors' offices, according to the girl in the woods. She walked down the row, scanning the neat, rectangular name tags until she came to DEIRDRE O'HANLON.

She knocked. A muffled voice from within said, "Come in!"

Of course, instead of a doorknob, another palm indentation. She sighed in frustration and knocked again. Her hand hurt. Plasteel-reinforced doors weren't designed to accommodate knuckles. After a moment, the door slid open. She stepped inside.

The office was small and completely uncluttered except for two red chairs. One was empty, the other occupied by a thin woman in vintage holo-clothing: flared blue jeans and a tight, floral-patterned long-sleeved shirt. The air was filled with externalized blueprints of some sort, close-up schematics full of intersecting lines and tiny white text. One of the blueprints extended upward from her palm. The woman slid a block of text from one side of the image to the other, then plucked it intact from her palm and gave it a gentle nudge. It glided over the empty chair to join a dozen more flat schematics gathered against the wall. She turned and smiled blankly at Mistletoe.

"Forgive me if I don't recognize you from any of my classes here—are you a Unison-only student?"

"You're Deirdre O'Hanlon?"

Her eyes scanned Mistletoe's face and clothing. She kept her smile. "If you need to discuss financial aid, you'll have to shimmer into the administration complex."

Mistletoe pulled the half-burned ESCU database from her pocket and held it out silently.

Deirdre gave a delighted chuckle. "I haven't seen one of those in years! Where on earth did you get it?"

"Listen to me. Jiri's dead. I think Aunt Dita is too." Mistletoe fought sudden, uncontrollable tears. "I don't want"—her eyes blurred—"I don't want anyone else to die because of who I am."

Deirdre sat stunned, mouth open. All of her externalized plans vapored away. The two of them stared at each other across the empty room.

"And who are you?" Deirdre whispered, pale and hesitant, like someone who knew what was coming and yet couldn't quite believe it.

"Fifteen years ago, you and Jiri and Dita and whoever else came and snatched me out of some UniCorp lab. I dream about it. There were gunshots."

"*Ma buh.* . . ." Deirdre swallowed and gestured to the empty chair. "Please, have a seat."

"I'll stand." Mistletoe felt a surprising surge of hostility toward this stranger, simply for being alive and comfortable while other people fought and died below the canopy.

"You have to understand," Deirdre said slowly and carefully. "It's been so long since I've been part of that world. These are names I haven't heard in a long time. Jiri . . ." She shook her head as if amazed by the two syllables of his name.

"He died right in front of me," Mistletoe said coldly.

"Then we're still paying in blood." Deirdre looked past Mistletoe at the wall. "There was another one of us who never made it out of the lab."

"P."

Deirdre's eyes flicked back to Mistletoe's face. "Yes. Pyotr was my husband. How did you know?"

"Jiri's notes."

"He kept notes? With *names*?"

"Just the first letters. I blew them up." She softened the threatening edge in her voice. "Sorry about your husband."

Deirdre's eyes drifted to the blank wall once again. "Fifteen years ago, I was such an idealist. We all were. Especially Pyotr—he was a dreamer. Dita used to say that he lived half inside this world and half inside the world he *wanted*, the one where the canopy had never existed, where Unison was open to everybody. The rest of us were a bit more pragmatic." She laughed. "But Pyotr . . ."

Mistletoe watched the tiny muscles in Deirdre's face twitch, relax, then twitch again as she remembered some specific, long-buried detail. Her mouth curled into the tiniest of smiles.

"He used to say about you, Anna—"

"It's Mistletoe now."

"Mistletoe . . ." Deirdre considered this. "Pretty name. Pyotr used to say we should all be willing to die in order to win your freedom. Then he went and did it."

"I didn't ask him to—I didn't ask for any of this."

"But here you are." Now it was Deirdre who hardened her tone. "I couldn't even bury him, you know. We were all running. Jiri had you in his arms. Pyotr was convinced the other subject, the boy, was somewhere inside. Associates were swarming. We'd lost our only advantage, surprise. Maybe if one of us had gone with him . . ." She was gripping her knees hard, the blood drained from her long, elegant fingers. "But I ran. I didn't want to die."

She flipped her palm. A grainy picture of a man's face appeared in the air. He had long black hair that fell in wisps in front of his eyes, a sharp nose, and small, serious lips pursed in deep contemplation.

"That's him," Deirdre said, shoving the image forward. "My husband."

Mistletoe imagined this man, along with Jiri, Deirdre, and Aunt Dita, all sitting around a cramped shanty, arguing, laughing, listening to music. It was strange to think of Jiri—*especially* Jiri—as a young man with friends.

"What were you, some kind of gang?"

Deirdre vapored away the picture. "Bombs were our thing. We were young enough to believe that blowing a hole in the canopy would spark a revolution." She lifted her arms in mock exultation. "Then Magnus and Ivor came to us with classified information about UniCorp, the great shining beacon of topside power. Two experimental subjects. Of course, they couldn't tell us what you were for. Only that you were important to Martin Truax. And for us, back then, that was enough."

"The boy's free now," Mistletoe said. "His name is Ambrose." She thought about adding, *So your husband didn't die for no reason*—but recognized that it sounded cheap and shabby and would offer little comfort.

Deirdre nodded. Then, reluctantly, she coaxed out a careful sentence: "I think . . . I think he came to see me."

Mistletoe had to stop herself from grabbing Deirdre by the shoulders. "He was *here*?"

"No." She began to make nervous, twisting finger sculptures with her hands. "I shouldn't be telling you this. I've never told anyone. In Unison, I switch between a few different IDs, but I use a specific one for my business. A teenager, a girl, like you. Application industry people let down their guard if they think they're dealing with someone young and naive. And it's just . . . nice to be a girl again, for a little while.

"Anyway, one of my gamer contacts brought me a new user named Adam Trevor with some pretty heavy questions. He's into furniture design and singing pop songs."

"That's not him. I told you, his name's Ambrose. And all he cares about is his dumb job."

She put up a hand. "That's my point: it was obvious he wasn't who he said he was. Fake login, fake Profile, just like mine. And he was chasing intel on Unison 3.0."

"Did he say where he was going?"

"Nowhere. He freaked out. His Thoughtstream *hurt*, like it had been overloaded with a million new Friends at once. And the look on his face—it was like he was stuck in a nightmare. It was enough to convince me to stay out for a while. Let the upgrade sort itself out, let Martin do whatever he's going to do. I'll go back when it stabilizes."

"But Ambrose needs help."

"What am I supposed to do? I'm an ESCU professor now. I have a life up here."

"So get me logged in."

"You want to help him? The best thing you can do is disappear. Leave the city and stay out of Unison."

"If I run away and he dies, then I'll be—" She caught herself.

"Finish it."

"Never mind."

Deirdre's voice was coated in ice. "Finish what you were going to say."

Mistletoe put her hands on her hips. "If I run away and he dies, I'll be just like you, talking about the things I should've done when I had the chance."

Deirdre's mouth quivered once. She nodded almost imperceptibly, then turned in her chair and slid her palm along the blank wall beside her. A rectangular panel slid open to reveal several orange jars. Deirdre selected one and unscrewed the cap. She pulled out a clear gelatin capsule the size of her thumb and tossed it to Mistletoe.

"What's this?"

The capsule was teeming with life forms, tiny silver and black bugs that scuttled like minuscule versions of Sliv's camera-insect.

"It's an early prototype of a nonhardcoded login device I'm helping to develop."

Mistletoe peered at the little bug colony. "Gross."

"It's our first attempt, so it's a very basic, one-time-use login. You'll be able to move through Unison, but you won't have a Profile or Thoughtstream. It won't respond to your presence. You can't make Friends. Press your palms against your temples when you're ready to shimmer out. That's how it's supposed to work."

"You mean you don't know?" The capsule bounced and rattled in her hand. She almost dropped it.

"It's never been tested."

"And you're gonna drill this thing into my *hand*?"

"No, nothing like that," Deirdre assured her. "You just eat it."

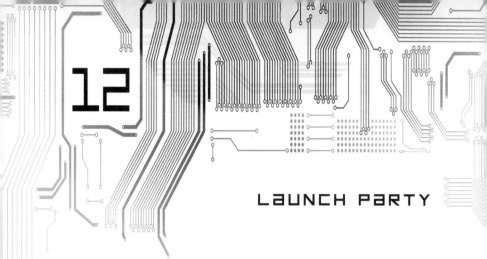

12

LAUNCH PARTY

AMBROSE SCREAMED his way down the chute, which descended through the walls of the UniCorp building at unpredictable angles. He tried to keep his mouth shut, but the sharp changes in direction, plus his dangerous velocity through complete darkness, seemed to pull the terrified yelps from his lungs. And yet, despite the stomach-turning intensity of the ride, he maintained one clear thought: Len had managed to operate a rogue security force and undermine his own father's plans, all while maintaining his cover as the Perfect Bureaucrat. And he had risked—and lost—everything to do it for Ambrose.

The chute gave way to empty space. He stopped sliding and started falling.

His scream hung in the air all around him, then trailed up the chute. He exhaled a sharp *hrrrmmpphhhh* as he landed butt-first against something soft, but not *that* soft.

Temperfoam. He sank into its folds as they formed a soft shell around him. Then the foam gave way, depositing him into a pile of sheets and pillows on the floor of a closet-sized room lit by a single lamp. Ambrose stood up and took a few deep breaths to slow his racing heart. He calculated the rate of his fall and the approximate height of the building and determined that he was slightly below ground, at about the same level as Len's private entrance.

In front of him was a narrow opening in the wall. Another short trip through a mercifully horizontal tunnel, and he found himself in a cramped, rough-hewn space containing a black UniCorp security car. He took a moment to run his hand along the smooth, rounded top that curved back to meet the under-carriage in a single gleaming point. He slid the door open.

"Thanks, big brother."

As soon as he sat down, the ceiling of the makeshift garage opened to expose a clear, pink dawn breaking over Eastern Seaboard City. The car door closed. The console blinked to life. His brother had programmed autopilot for a preplanned route.

The triple-coiled ion lifts engaged, and the car shot up out of its underground parking space, perfectly timing its jump to seamlessly enter the lowest traffic flow. Ambrose slid down in his seat as the car joined the earliest stage of the Fleshbound Parade. This would be the perfect opportunity to sleep, if only his body were capable of doing so. He closed his eyes and rubbed his aching temples. Maybe if he just cleared his mind, he could drift away for a minute or two. Maybe he could even learn to simulate the effects of sleep, perform his own sort of calibration to keep himself sane.

His hands stopped when they felt the wires. A dozen of them, maybe more, snaking out from the skin of his face and curling down to his lap. He bolted upright and gasped, *"Reflection."*

The window glass became a mirror. He stared at himself, pale and drawn, hands clutching the sides of his face.

There weren't any wires. His face was made of normal human flesh.

The car jumped to an upper traffic flow. He was headed north, blazing through the New England Expansion. He sat upright, taking deep, measured breaths, trying to maintain control over his wayward mind. He was haunted by the thought that his time was running out; if he didn't find a way to calibrate, the procedure would turn him into a drooling, paranoid lunatic. It would be worse than dying, because any rare moment of lucidity could remind him of the sane person he used to be. Fleeting memories of a blue pigtail, a subcanopy adventure, a friend from another life.

He diminished the mirror and looked out the window to distract himself, the scene a series of jumpy flashes, soaked in radiant morning light.

Glittering tops of half-submerged luxury apartment domes in Providence Harbor.

The massive green-sided atmoscraper of the Boston Heights Fenway Sports Conglomerate headquarters.

The Maine Corridor's impossibly winding but sparse traffic flow.

Finally, he was cruising alone near the Canadian border, leaving the northern outskirts of ESC—ancient concrete warehouses huddled beneath squat ten-story apartment buildings—to sputter out sadly in his wake. The security car slowed alongside a dense pine forest, then swung a hard left down a tree-lined path. Spiny branches clawed at the windows as the trail narrowed and disappeared.

The car stopped in a small clearing, where it signaled and linked to some hidden receiver. A hole opened up in the earth. The car eased inside and set down gently. Ambrose crawled out and stretched. Above him, the ground closed. A dim light blinked on.

He was inside a subterranean room made of packed dirt. Gnarled roots snaked along the walls. A ragged green armchair slumped in the corner.

His own personal shimmerdome, hidden deep in the wilderness, but still close enough to the Maine Corridor to latch on to a signal. Len had understood that Martin and his unlimited resources would hold a tight grip on the fleshbound world. Ambrose could get lucky and escape over and over again, but he would always be a rat in a maze. In Unison, at least he'd be in a position to—what did Len say?—throw himself into the gears.

He sat in the chair. With his eyes closed he began to wonder about Mistletoe, where she was, if she was okay. He thought about how she had pushed him against the side of the subcanopy elevator for insulting her neighborhood.

Deep breath. The damp, earthy smell of the room reminded him of her scented pigtail. How pungent it had been, mashed against his face as he rode behind her on that tiny death-trap scoot! If his mind was going to decay into a nonsensical patchwork of memories and hallucinations, he hoped some of them would be of Mistletoe. He slapped his palms together and shimmered.

His throat tickled, but he couldn't cough.

He tasted the hot-penny tang of battery acid.

The dim light snuffed out, and he felt himself lift off the chair.

Ecstasy surged through him; his troubles were distant and meaningless. He was home.

He emerged from the cave into the ragged edge of Unison's ESC bitmapping. Roots twisted and rumbled beneath his feet. An apple orchard sprang up around him. Some of the trees bent and reshaped into unique chairs and tables. Intricate hand-carved patterns emerged in the grain of the wood. He ran his hand along the deep, spiraled carvings in the side of a strange, T-shaped chair. At one end of the top crossbar was a little door with a handle shaped like a perched owl.

His Feed said:

Suburban mailbox, mid-twentieth century.

So it wasn't a chair at all—it was one of those antique inboxes for paper correspondence. He watched as it lacquered itself, the glossy finish running from top to bottom. It was breathtakingly beautiful. He had always loved furniture, ever since he was a little boy, and never thought it possible for that love to grow. It was simply a fixed part of him, like his hands and feet and heart. But now, for the first time, surrounded by all this beauty, his entire being swelled with—

Wait. Something was wrong. He accessed his Profile.

My name is Adam Trevor.

He relaxed and strolled through the orchard, kicking at the brittle leaves that coated the soft path beneath his feet. Nothing was wrong. He was Adam Trevor, and he was home. But still, something nagged at him, a gnawing anxiety like he had missed a meeting.

Where did he work?

He didn't. That was impossible. He was fifteen years old. He wanted to be a singer someday, but—

He viewed his Friends: Takashi Nakamura and Sonia Carter. It was good to have Friends. Why did he only have two? That wasn't in the spirit of Unison. Well, now that he was home, he could devote some time to Friending new people.

He admired the patches of light that pooled on the leafy trail beneath his feet. It was so peaceful here. He felt as if he could lie down in a bed of dry leaves and curl up forever. The orchard began to thin out. A wooden archway covered in apple blossoms marked the edge.

Suddenly, he felt a twitch in the back of his mind. It was uncomfortable for a second—an itch he couldn't scratch—but then his Feed said:

Takashi Nakamura is in Unison!

His First Friend's Thoughtstream blinked to life.

Takashi Nakamura just became a level 65 General in the Saturnine War RPG.

Adam Trevor felt the afterglow of Takashi's achievement. His First Friend was proud, and he felt bits and pieces of Takashi's fulfillment like the warm patches of light through the trees. Everyone was so happy today! He laughed out loud.

At the very edge of the orchard he stopped. Before him, ghosts were lining up behind a red velvet rope. Their heavy Thoughtstream chatter blindsided him: they were each desperate to be his Friend. The line ended beneath the marquee of a grand brick concert hall. Red letters on the marquee said:

UNICORP AUDITORIUM PRESENTS AN EVENING WITH ADAM TREVOR

It didn't make total sense, but he thought he could vaguely remember the grueling audition process, the heartbreak of rejection, the late nights and long hours spent with a voice coach. He deserved this, after all his hard work. He'd finally made it! This concert was his shot at superstardom.

A single door opened a few feet down from the front entrance. A ghost with a plump face and shiny, slicked-back hair leaned out and said, "Psst! Mr. Trevor! We've been waiting for you—this way!"

Ambrose ran to the door marked ARTISTS' ENTRANCE and ducked inside a dim backstage hallway. The ghost was short, round, and impeccably dressed in a tuxedo. He bowed.

"It is my great pleasure to finally meet you. If you'll follow me, I'll take you to the stage for your sound check."

He pulled back a maroon velvet curtain. The stage was empty except for a piano and a microphone.

"I play the piano," Adam said.

The man smiled. "Of course you do. And it's a full house tonight, so you'd better warm up. Please." The man extended his hand to indicate the empty auditorium. Adam walked onstage, his footsteps echoing inside the cavernous space.

I am Adam Trevor. I play the piano. I am Adam Trevor. I sing.

He sat on the wooden bench and plunked a white key with

his left hand. The low tone sounded ominous, a rumble from the deep. He plinked out a chirpy three-note melody with his right. Then he combined them both, improvising a song about a mean old storm cloud that Friends a chipmunk.

A girl's hand grabbed his wrist before he could resolve a particularly brilliant chord progression. He looked up from the piano. She was familiar—and pretty, despite her ragged fashion sense—maybe an old fan or someone he knew from his performing arts middle school?

"Don't quit your day job," she said.

Somehow, her voice reminded him of a recent dream: a frantic escape, a journey north, a hole in the middle of the woods.

"How did you get in here?"

"Ambrose," she said, "what's wrong with you?"

All around the girl, shadows in the auditorium deepened and crept along the stage floor. He looked out at the rows of empty red seats, barely lit by the round lights in the domed ceiling above. This place was starting to make him uneasy.

"It's me—Mistletoe!" She whipped a fluffy blue pigtail over her shoulder. He got a powerful whiff of pungent spices and coughed.

He thought he remembered the first time they met. Yes: it had been in a subcanopy alley. But why would he have been in a neighborhood like that?

She gave him a rough shake. "Your name is Ambrose Truax. We escaped from those two cops together. The creepy old brothers caught us. Magnus and Ivor, remember? Then we got split up. You're *Ambrose*."

He slid off the bench and backed away slowly, shaking his

head. "My name is Adam," he mumbled. "I'm supposed to sing tonight. I have to warm up." His words felt wrong, like someone else was broadcasting from his mouth.

The lights went down in the auditorium. Harsh whispers came from the seats.

"We have to get out of here," she said.

"This is where I belong," he said weakly. "I'm happy here." But he didn't believe it. He didn't know where he belonged.

Mistletoe tugged at his sleeve. Voices rained down from the darkened rows of seats.

"Sing!"

"Come on, Adam, play for us!"

"We love you!"

Mistletoe said, "Don't listen." She wrenched his arm and yanked him off the piano bench. He waved to his unseen fans as she dragged him back through the velvet curtain.

"Are we Friends?" he asked. He had the creeping sensation that she didn't like him very much.

"Not in here."

They burst out the ARTISTS' ENTRANCE door and into the bright sunlight. He followed her away from the UniCorp Auditorium and up a hill covered in tall grass that swished against his legs. At the top of the hill was a gathering of pine trees. She led him into the shady center and sat next to him on a wide, many-ringed stump.

"Listen to me." She held his hand. "Your name is Ambrose Truax. You wear holo-suits and smell like Brussels. We met in Little Saigon, where everything looks old to you. I have a scoot named Nelson."

Dizziness clouded his vision. He felt nauseated.

"The cops chased us, but we got away."

He closed his eyes and saw himself riding behind Mistletoe on the back of a rickety scoot. They cruised along a narrow, uneven street at the top of a shanty-stack. The underside of the canopy was a few feet above their heads. Her long blue pigtail tickled his nose. His arms were wrapped around her warm stomach, and it made him happy to be close to her. And then he remembered.

She saved my life. My name—

The scene blinked to a dank, cavernous lab strewn with the guts of pre-Unison machinery. A white-haired man who smelled like mold leaned in close and gripped his wrist tight. The man pushed a single sharp prong through his hand. Pain sliced up his arm. He remembered:

The old man hardcoded a new ID. My name is—

Blink. He was crouched behind a scan-tube next to someone holding a disruptor, someone very familiar who was screaming at him to run.

Blink. A marble hung suspended in the thin air between ESC atmoscrapers, spinning forever on its axis.

My name is Ambrose.

He remembered everything.

"My name is Ambrose Truax!" he said as his mind returned to the clearing in the middle of the pines. He gazed around, wide-eyed. "Wow," he said. Deep breath. "Okay. The Adam Trevor ID was perfectly in sync with Unison. It completely overshadowed my own consciousness. And it was immediate—as soon as I shimmered in, I lost myself."

He stood up from the stump and did a quick mental status check. He was dismayed to find that the urge to run back inside the concert hall and sing for his adoring fans was still tugging at his mind, enticing him. But at least he could recognize the impulse and try to ignore it. He paced, repeating his real name to himself.

"My name is Ambrose Truax. My name is Ambrose Truax. My name is—"

"You know you're saying that out loud, right?" Mistletoe looked around at all the perfectly designed Unison pine trees. "This place is friending *weird,* by the way. Nice work."

It occurred to Ambrose that he had no idea if this user was really Mistletoe. She wasn't a ghost, but she wasn't his Friend either. And he couldn't get a fix on her Profile or Thoughtstream. According to Unison, she didn't exist.

"How did you get here? The Mistletoe I know doesn't even have topside access, much less a Unison ID."

She jumped up and jabbed a finger into his chest. That pretty much convinced him that he was dealing with the right girl.

"First, how about *Thanks for saving my ass again*? What's that, like, the millionth time since we met? And second, nice to see you, too."

He put up his hands. "Okay, sorry, but you have to understand, I haven't been thinking straight since I saw you last. I've been seeing things. I left Magnus and Ivor's to try to get calibrated, but . . . seriously, how *did* you get here?"

"Professor Deirdre O'Hanlon."

"Who?"

"I think when you met her she was some kind of"—she snapped her fingers, trying to think—"Application builder."

He paused. "Sonia Carter."

"Her real name's Deirdre," Mistletoe said. "She's a professor of Unison junk at ESC University. I found out about her from Jiri's notes."

"Wait—you were at ESCU? How'd you get topside?"

"I know this one boy . . ." She trailed off like she was waiting for a reaction. Ambrose wasn't sure what he was supposed to say.

"Huh."

"Who got me past the airlock. And then Deirdre helped me log in."

"Implanted you." He tapped his palm.

She shook her head. "I wish. I had to swallow a giant pill full of bugs."

Explains why you're off the grid, he thought. "Do you have any idea how friending unsafe that is?" The subcanopy slang rolled off his tongue like he'd grown up with it. "Swallowing some back-alley biotech login? Those bugs are in your *brain* now. You can't do stuff like this. I don't want to—" He silenced himself.

"Don't want to what?"

"I don't want to lose you again."

Despite the chaotic nature of his current brain functions, he was certain of this one truth. He had the overwhelming urge to lay a finger against the side of her neck, to feel her pulse and the smoothness of her skin all at once. Real skin, Unison skin, it didn't matter.

She seemed taken aback.

"Ambrose," she said, "no one's ever . . ." For the first time since they met, she dropped her subcanopy street armor. "I've never . . ." Her smile was sad and somehow very old. She tried again. "I wish I'd known you before all this."

His heart pounded. And then his Thoughtstream crackled:

Takashi Nakamura is psyched to see his Friend sing tonight!

He could feel Takashi's presence crawling over his skin, suffocatingly happy like an overmedicated patient.

"Oh, no," he said. "Brace yourself."

Takashi burst into the clearing, breathless and red-faced. Ambrose waited for him to mention their strange and abrupt good-bye in the stadium. His First Friend gestured wildly toward a gap between the trees.

"What are you doing hiding, Adam? Haven't you seen it out there? It's beautiful!" His Mood-shadow wrapped wriggling orange tendrils around his legs and waist.

"Yick," Mistletoe said, stepping back.

"Nice to meet you!" Takashi said.

"Hi," she managed weakly, eyeing the Mood-shadow's twisting vines with distaste.

Takashi Nakamura is 011010000110111101101101100101.

Ambrose waved a hand in front of his Friend's face. "Um, Takashi?"

Takashi looked straight through Ambrose to the other side of the clearing. Then he giggled distantly. "You ever—you ever just see how all the layers of the world fit together? And how they're for all your Friends and for you *at the same time*? It's like you're the simplest nano, okay?" He pinched his thumb and forefinger together to demonstrate the tiny size. "And you're dedicated to this one repetitive function—back and forth or up and down—and at the same time you're this"—he waved his arms, struggling to convey the blissful understanding racing around his brain—"*pinwheel of Friendship*!" he said triumphantly.

Ambrose pointed at the Mood-shadow, which was reacting to Takashi's profound happiness by climbing up his chest and wrapping around his neck.

"Is that supposed to happen? I mean, are you . . ."

"I'm finally *me*, Adam! I'm everything I ever wanted to be."

Warily, they followed Takashi through the trees and out into the sunlight. Beginning at the foot of the hill was a vast field that stretched toward the hazy skyline of bitmapped ESC. The field was populated by millions of users swaying and jostling together in groups like tightly packed schools of fish, which gave Ambrose the alarming feeling that he was looking out across the floor of a waterless ocean. It took a few speechless minutes for him to realize that the users were milling about with a purpose, a slow forward progress that dragged them toward a looming monstrosity that threatened to blot out the perfect Unison sun.

"Greymatter," Ambrose said.

"Told you it was beautiful!" Takashi yelled over his shoulder as he ran down the hill.

Martin's estate was the size of a city. New additions sprawled from both sides, the stacked glass and intertwined chrome of modern atmoscrapers dwarfing the original Victorian manor.

The expansion crept along the perimeter of the field, a sparkling twenty-first-century subdivision enclosing the mass of users like two giant claws.

As the users reached the front of the estate, their figures decomposed; months of decay happened in a sickening instant. From the bodily wreckage of each user, raw data unwound in colorful skeins that slithered into the walls of the house.

The estate was consuming Profile information.

"Is that good or bad?" Mistletoe asked.

Ambrose's Feed screamed:

Congratulations! You've been selected to participate in a free trial of Unison 3.0 (Beta Version). Please attend our launch party at Greymatter!

Ambrose turned to Mistletoe but was struck dumb by sudden, white-hot flares of joy that knifed through his Thoughtstream. In an instant, Unison compressed the distance between his own Thoughtstream and those of his fellow users. Now they all seemed to originate in the same place, deep within his own mind, like a deafening echo chamber.

Lauren Jenkins **loves her Friends more than anything else in the whole world! :)**

Julia Pittman **became a fan of Adam Trevor.**

Oscar Ward **thinks that life is about relaxing and just ENJOYING everything!**

Chris Riley wonders why it took him so long to realize how easy it is to be happy.

Mark Sullivan ;) ;) ;) ;) ;)

Millions of full, detailed Profiles began to invade his Feed. And they were all inviting him to one Event: Launch Party at Greymatter.

It was going to be so much fun.

Maybe he could even play a few songs for all his new Friends.

He started down the hill. Someone tugged at his sleeve: the girl from the auditorium. She'd interrupted his preshow warm-up, and now she was trying to stop him from attending the Launch Party. He pulled away from her—crazy stalker!—and was about to tell her to leave him alone when her entire body jolted backward, as if she'd accidentally dropped a knife and was trying to keep it from landing on her foot. Her gaze became vacant and detached. Her mouth dropped open. Then she glitched and blinked out of existence.

No great loss. She hadn't been his Friend, anyway.

He joined the users in the field and made his way toward the estate, whistling happily and enjoying the feel of the sun on his face.

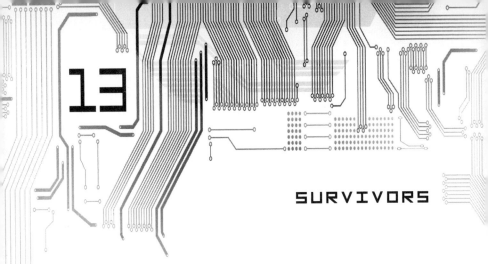

13

SURVIVORS

SHE WAS FLOATING in darkness. The tube slid open. A light shone down. She squinted. A man's silhouette leaned in front of the light, blocking the sun-bright center but not the glow. Her eyes adjusted. The crisp angles of a neat suit and tie appeared within the dark space, then the silhouette disappeared. The bright ball of light returned.

Out of sight, men spoke in hushed tones punctuated by an occasional wet *thwack*. She felt herself tilt forward with a low mechanical *whirrrr* and gradually became aware that she was in a room filled with long metal tubes. The tube across from her was tilted upright and open. Inside was a tiny squirming baby with long wires protruding from his head. He looked straight at her and froze. She tried to wave, but her arms were strapped down. Instead, she gurgled her best greeting. He blinked and moved his lips.

Once again: *thwack*.

Her eyes tracked the noise past the other baby's tube to the back of the room, where two men in white lab coats and a third man—the one who had peeked at her—bent over a long table, poking and prodding a fleshy mound. The third man stood up and said something to the other two, then picked up the mound. Silver wires dangled from the limp thing. Then a tiny arm.

It was a baby—just like her and the boy in the other tube. Except it wasn't moving. The third man held the baby steady as he snapped off one of the wires and held it up to the light. He turned it over in his hands, studying it from every angle. He shook his head. The two men in lab coats stood motionless as the third man tossed the baby into a clear cylindrical tank filled with green fluid and the lifeless, floating bodies of a dozen other babies, their wires snaking around each other, buoyed by a slight current.

The baby displaced another with a wet *thwack*.

She transferred her helpless gaze to the boy across from her, who was staring back with his mouth hanging open and a thick string of drool dangling from his lower lip.

"Gahh," he said.

She tried to point at the men, but she couldn't move, and anyway he couldn't turn around to see what was happening.

Instead, she screamed.

The scene retreated to the end of a long tunnel and dissolved. Then it rushed forward and became Professor Deirdre O'Hanlon's high, pale forehead and wide green eyes, inches from her own.

Mistletoe tried to move. Her arms were still pinned. How was that possible? The white walls and red chairs of the spartan ESCU office appeared at the edge of her vision.

"Ambrose!" Mistletoe screamed, struggling against the leaden force pinning her wrists. "Don't go down there!" The sides of her head felt hot and slick with sweat.

"Calm down," Deirdre said. "He can't hear you. You're with me again."

The professor tightened her grip, mashing Mistletoe's palms against her temples until her head ached.

She'd been extracted.

Mistletoe wriggled away. "Put me back in."

"Can't do that. They're here." Deirdre flipped her palm. An externalized image of the ESCU building's lobby appeared. UniCorp Security Associates lined the two walkways that crossed above the glass box, aiming their disruptors downward in quick, graceful sweeps. On the floor, a second team of Associates examined a row of students whose externalized ESCU ID spheres glittered above their upturned palms.

"Building security feed," Deirdre said.

Mistletoe watched the soundless video as a student stepped forward and extinguished his ID. He yelled something at the nearest Associate, his enraged mouth working silently, and received a swift crack on the side of the head with the blunted tip of a disruptor. The boy crumpled into a crooked line on the floor. Next to him, the red-haired girl who had given Mistletoe chocolate and directions presented her ID for inspection. A Security Associate passed his hand through the iridescent sphere and moved down the row.

Mistletoe felt the weight of her own disruptor wrapped around her forearm, dormant inside her sleeve. She fought the crazy urge to close her fist, arm the weapon, and burst through the office door, blasting away. *Looking for me, guys?*

Another group of Associates stepped into view and began dispersing along the perimeter of the room, taking positions in front of the professors' offices, two men to a door.

Deirdre dismissed the image and pulled a bulging mud-colored duffel bag from behind the chair.

"I thought this might happen someday," she said, whisking the orange jars and loose capsules from the rectangular wall slot into the bag.

"Nobody followed me here," Mistletoe said.

Deirdre shouldered the bag, then grabbed the red chair by its rounded armrest and threw it aside with brisk authority. The newly exposed segment of wall was bare except for another indented palm print.

"It's my fault for giving you the login. I took a stupid risk with experimental technology, and now we have to run."

Mistletoe felt rooted to the spot by a cold, achy sickness that crept down her neck into her chest and stomach. That's exactly what she was: *experimental technology*. Ivor had been right about the danger of being abruptly disconnected from Unison: horrible memories, deeply suppressed, were relived in acute detail.

"You don't understand," Mistletoe said. "He's lost in there without me."

Deirdre fit her hand into the indentation. A horizontal crack appeared in the back wall and widened to reveal the ESCU campus. The forest was brushed with long stripes of afternoon sunlight. Mistletoe squinted as a sunbeam scored a direct hit into Deirdre's office.

"My priority right now is not being shot," Deirdre said, hoisting one leg storklike through the rectangular opening in the wall and fluidly slipping the rest of her body out of the room. "Yours should be, too."

Mistletoe almost pointed out the capsule that slipped from

the side pouch of the professor's bag as she pulled it through behind her. Instead, she reached down and scooped it up, slipping it into her pocket as she climbed out and landed in the soft grass beside the gray monument. She turned to survey the campus and found herself staring down the bright orange barrel of an armed disruptor. The weapon was attached to a man wearing a shapeless brown hat, bobbing gently on his idling ESCPD scoot. Next to him, his redheaded partner brandished an identical disruptor, rather than the nonlethal stunner baton he'd used during their subcanopy chase.

Mistletoe clenched her fist. The disruptor slid out from beneath her sleeve and closed around her hand. She thumbed it to full power and tried to hold her arm steady.

Hat licked his chapped lips. It was strange to see him do something so natural and human. Mistletoe wondered if these men had families at home, wives and kids for whom they'd tell the exciting story of hunting two fugitive kids. She pictured them sitting down to a dinner of juicy roast chicken and whatever topside people got out of those silver boxes.

Red nodded at her disruptor, which had turned a sickly shade of yellow as it struggled to maintain the full-power charge. "Might be time for a tune-up."

Mistletoe waited for Deirdre to reveal the high-tech weapon she surely had hidden beneath her shirt and say something like *This oughta even things up a bit.* She glanced sideways at the professor, who was just standing there, hands up next to her head to show they were empty.

Hat sniffed the air. "You smell that?"

Mistletoe didn't smell anything, but she got a hint of the stopped-clock feeling she'd had on Aunt Dita's street in the seconds before the explosion. The eerie stillness of that moment seemed to infect the two cops, so that even their scoots hung motionless in the air.

Time sped up with two quick glints of silver, followed by two wet, choking sounds:

Shlurnk. Shlurnk.

Red's nondisruptor hand went to his throat, while Hat just slumped in his seat, gasping for breath, twitching like a frantic rabbit. Mistletoe and Deirdre backed against the stone wall. Embedded in each man's neck was a circle of metal shark's teeth.

Mistletoe turned away. She didn't want to see the final slackening of their features. It was too much like Jiri's last moment. The leaves of a nearby tree rustled, catching her attention. Feet dangled, legs appeared, and then an entire boy hung for a moment before dropping to the ground.

Sliv.

He moved soundlessly toward them across the grass. He was wearing a long-sleeved shirt decorated in blobs of green and brown: vintage camouflage. Slung across his chest was a leather bandolier hung with several more homemade shurikens, stumpy blades soldered between the blunted teeth of silver gears. He'd covered his missing hand with a worn brown glove. Flashing Mistletoe a tight smile, he began struggling to pull Hat's limp body from the sleek black scoot.

"Little help?" he said. Mistletoe sprang forward and pushed from the other side, careful not to trigger her disruptor, which she kept armed, just in case. Together they managed to slide Hat off his seat and into Sliv's arms. The cop's crisp tan shirt untucked and ruffled up about his chin, covering the wound in his neck.

"Thanks for not listening to me," Mistletoe said, once they'd propped Hat against the stone wall.

"How'd I know you'd get into trouble up here?"

Deirdre placed Red's body alongside his partner's, efficiently patting down his pockets and transferring his stunner baton to her bag. "Old habit," she said, straightening up.

Mistletoe wondered if Deirdre was closer to her past than she'd like to think. Deirdre hopped up onto Red's scoot and shifted her bag into her lap. "If we head north," she said, "there's a retreat for tenured professors just outside Montreal."

"They'll look for you there," Mistletoe said.

"I'm not tenured."

"Forget that," Sliv said, hoisting himself up onto Hat's scoot. "I got a safe place back home." He extended a hand and swung Mistletoe up onto the seat.

Deirdre pointed to the ground. "Back home, meaning subcanopy?"

"Yeah," Mistletoe said. She squeezed between Sliv and the control panel. "I'm driving."

The Watchmakers lazed around the emergency room of the abandoned Rio II hospital like dogs in the summertime, watching with half-open eyes and sleepy curiosity as Sliv escorted his two guests through their hideout. They'd taken sea green mattresses from the hospital beds and used them to pad a labyrinthine warren of connected bunks that stretched along the chipped and peeling walls of the ER. Some gang members had hung plaid sheets and colorful tapestries for curtains, while others lounged around in their underwear in full view of everyone else. Even, Mistletoe noticed with surprise, some of the girls. With an indignant flare, she wondered why Sliv had never asked her to join.

A sudden skittering noise beside them made Deirdre freeze. The camera-insect crested a small hill of rusted industrial coffee makers and trained its lens on the visitors. Sliv waved it away, and the insect disappeared beneath the bunk of a snoring boy with shockingly white hair.

"You don't have to stay out here with us," Sliv said. "I'll get a decent place put together for you in one of the surgical wards."

It had taken them several hours to get to the hospital. First Sliv had directed them through a head-spinning network of topside alleys to make sure they weren't being followed. Then they had abandoned the ESCPD scoots at the airlock before climbing down the access shaft and taking a long, circuitous route through a series of narrow tunnels that deposited them in the emergency room.

"Early bedtime around here," Deirdre said.

"We forage at night," Sliv explained. "It's almost time to wake up."

At the back of the ER, behind a desk that said PLEASE SIGN IN, Sliv pulled off his glove and unbuttoned his camouflage shirt. He reached down to unbutton his pants, then seemed to remember that he had company.

" 'Scuse me," he said, disappearing into an office behind the desk.

"This place is okay," Deirdre said. She almost sounded convinced. "It's good. You're better off down here."

An unmanned red vacuum cleaner rolled past, trailing a

long cord. It stopped next to the desk and lowered the trunk of a long attachment to suction up a gathering of steely gray lint, then retreated back down the corridor.

"Maybe not *here*, exactly," Deirdre said, staring at the newly cleaned spot on the tile floor. "But down below the canopy, out of signal range. As long as you keep moving."

"I plan to," Mistletoe said. She watched the vacuum cleaner disappear behind the skeletal teardrop-shaped chassis of a topside car and wondered if Sliv had kept Nelson intact, or if the scoot had already been gutted for spare parts.

"So describe your Unison experience," Deirdre said.

"Confusing and scary pretty much covers it."

"Give me specifics."

"I found Ambrose easy enough because the name he was using when you met him—"

"Adam Trevor."

"—was up on posters advertising a concert he was supposed to be playing. Except when I found him, he really thought he was Adam, like it wasn't a fake Profile anymore. He was making up a song about a cloud. I snapped him out of it, but that didn't last. So unless I get back in there to remind Ambrose who he is—"

"I can't let you do that."

"It's not up to you."

"Giving you that login was a mistake. I was right the first time: the best thing to do is run."

"I won't leave Ambrose. He wouldn't leave me."

"You don't know that. And since I spent fifteen years building a career you destroyed in the course of an afternoon, the least you can do is consider my advice."

Mistletoe studied the floor, located a dark smudge the vacuum had missed. She felt like a fairy-tale demon who flitted into people's lives and left behind wreckage. Her wrist brushed against the lump of the login capsule in her pocket. As soon as she could find an excuse to get away from the professor, she'd head for the only subcanopy signal she knew of.

"What else happened in there?" Deirdre asked. Mistletoe looked up. She noticed the wrinkles around the outside of the professor's eyes, the deep creases of worry etched into her forehead. Maybe survivors ended up weary and hollow; maybe Pyotr was the lucky one.

"Martin's big mansion was growing."

"You saw Greymatter?"

"Can't miss it. It's where everybody was going. Their Profiles were feeding it, or something."

Deirdre's eyes were someplace far away. "I always used to think people down here should fight to be allowed inside Unison, that we had a responsibility to help every human being share in the progress such a great social network represented. But toward the end Pyotr thought we were better off without it. He used to say, 'UniCorp is planting users like seeds, watching them grow, waiting for the harvest.'"

When the office door opened, Mistletoe turned gratefully to Sliv. He'd changed into a sleeveless black T-shirt and gray pants spattered with flecks of yellow and green paint.

"Lemme get the two of you settled before breakfast." He beckoned with the exposed metal of his left arm and started off down the hall.

Deirdre put her hand on Mistletoe's shoulder. "Pyotr was right."

Mistletoe shrugged her off and caught up with Sliv. "Is Nelson in one piece?"

"We fed it to the incinerator for kicks."

"Just because you saved my life doesn't mean I won't choke you."

Sliv pointed to a set of doors marked INTENSIVE CARE at the end of the hallway. "It's in there."

Mistletoe turned to face Deirdre, who was lagging a few steps behind. "Hey, can you give us a minute? We just want some time to catch up a little bit." She took Sliv's human hand and squeezed it tight, threading her fingers between his and pulling him close. He smelled like gasoline.

"Oh. I—I didn't realize," Deirdre said. "I'll just go get settled."

Mistletoe smiled. "Thanks. For everything."

"Surgical ward's around the corner," Sliv said as Mistletoe pulled him toward intensive care. "There's a shower and some beds. Take your pick."

Mistletoe pushed open the swinging doors. Inside the room Sliv pulled her against him and locked his hands around her waist. She bounced on her toes long enough to give him a dry peck on the cheek, then wriggled out of his embrace.

"That's for before," she said. "With the cops."

Sliv scratched the side of his chin, thinking. "So that was an act just now."

But Mistletoe was already making her way across the room, past a dozen scoots in various states of hopeless disrepair. Nelson was leaning up against the wall next to a hanging trellis of hammers, screwdrivers, and drills.

"Had to get the professor off my back," she said, running her hand along Nelson's torn seat.

Sliv followed her and clanged his silver gear hand against Nelson's nose. Startled, Mistletoe looked up at him.

"So that's it—half a kiss, and you're a ghost again." He folded his arms across his chest. "I really hope this guy is worth it."

"This isn't about a guy. What is it with you?"

He looked hurt. She reached for his hand but he brushed her off. "I'm not someone you have to lie to," he said.

"Okay." She took a deep breath. "There's a guy. But it's really not like that with him. Or, I don't know. It's hard to explain. He's just part of me."

Sliv made a face like he'd just had a long sip of sour milk.

"What about the girls here?" she asked quickly. "Do you ever . . ."

He scoffed. "Watchmakers have rules against that sort of thing. We're not a bunch of animals."

"I know. I didn't mean you were."

"Forget it." He pointed to her neck. "Guess you didn't like the necklace."

Her hand went to her collarbone. "I had to trade it to a cabbie for a ride."

"I hope he took you all the way to Iceland. The chain was real gold."

"Uh-huh. And the canopy's gonna rain mangoes."

"I'll show you a back way out of here if you promise me two things."

"Maybe and maybe."

"One: come back someday. Two: don't trade this for anything."

Using his human hand, he unclasped a bronze ring from the metal piston in his forearm and slid it onto Nelson's scuffed and rusted handlebar.

Without the guidance of the Chmura Dité, Mistletoe followed miles of damp, drippy, foul-smelling tunnels into dead ends and crumbling stations littered with twisted turnstiles. She tried not to think about how far gone Ambrose was going to be by the time she found him again and was fighting the urge to scream in frustration when she saw a distant pool of soft light leaking onto the tracks. She gunned Nelson and skidded around the corner, stopping just short of crashing into one of the leather couches in front of the old brothers' lab.

Inside, she leaned Nelson against a doorless refrigerator that smelled faintly of mustard and removed Sliv's ring from the handlebar. It was too big for her finger and too small for her wrist. The bronze was tarnished with fungal blotches of green. She slipped it into her pocket, where it fit snugly alongside Deirdre's capsule, and made her way to the open side of the hollow wire trunk that descended from the high, vaulted ceiling. The bucket of bloody rags was gone, along with the bank of monitors and keyboards. The wires that had pierced Ambrose's palms were dangling inside. She was glad that Magnus and Ivor weren't around. She didn't know if UniCorp could trace her login down here.

This place is their *home*, she reminded herself. What gave her the right to barge into people's lives and change them forever? She thought of Deirdre. Then she thought of Ambrose. She picked up one of the dangling implant wires and examined the tip, a triangular blade dabbed with dried blood.

"Planning a bit of surgery this evening?"

She dropped the wire and turned. Magnus and Ivor stood beneath the archway at the other end of the room. They had changed into charcoal gray robes, and Magnus was wearing a floppy, wide-brimmed hat that hid his face in shadow.

Ivor stepped into the room. "Funny how things change," he said with a surprising hint of good humor. Behind him, in the dim space beyond the archway, dark shapes shuffled and swayed.

"I know, I know," Mistletoe said. "You offered this to me, I ran away, and now I'm back."

Ivor said, "Remember, when you get one of those wires stuck through your palm, you'll still have to use that hand—and here I'd suggest wiping away the blood for a better grip—to stab the other one." He nudged Magnus. "Onward, brother."

They walked out from beneath the archway, followed by three furry brown beasts from the silent zoo, snorting and plodding along under the weight of the elaborate harnesses slung across their backs. When they were closer, Mistletoe noticed that each harness supported piles of equipment: monitors and keyboards from the lab, boxes stuffed with printed books and manuals, coils of insulated wire. She watched Magnus reach into his pocket for something the slobbery tongue of the creature behind him lapped up with one great lick.

"Puffed rice cereal," Magnus said. "I'm afraid you've picked a rather unfortunate time to visit, as we were just on our way out."

"I'm here on business," Mistletoe said. "I have this." She displayed the quivering capsule in the palm of her hand. "It's a one-time login. I just need a signal."

Magnus took off his hat, revealing matted wisps of white hair, and bent over for a better look. He poked it with a finger, then straightened up and turned to his brother.

"We truly are behind the times, Ivor."

"Hence the exile. As for you, our signal radiates. If you don't need to be hardcoded, all you need is proximity."

Mistletoe looked from Magnus to Ivor, deeply relieved that she didn't have to stab wires into her palms. "You're leaving?"

Ivor mopped his brow with a ragged strip of cloth. "Like I said, it's funny how things change."

Magnus replaced his hat on his head. "This is no longer our fight—hasn't been for years. It's time for us to step aside and leave things to you and Ambrose."

"My brother's change of heart can be traced back to the instant I paralyzed him with a police weapon," Ivor said. "Anyway, whatever happens, we'll be so far underground that we won't care."

"He doesn't mean that," Magnus said.

Ivor began leading the row of pack animals toward the door that led to the subway tunnels. "Yes I do," he called back. "I'm officially retired."

"Sorry about that kick," Mistletoe yelled after him.

He replied with a piercing single-note whistle. The goat-dog bounded across the floor from some unseen place and slid to a stop in front of Mistletoe.

"Hi, Patricia," Mistletoe said, receiving a gentle nuzzle from the animal's curved horn. Ivor whistled a second time. Patricia looked at Mistletoe expectantly, then trotted to his side.

Magnus tipped the brim of his hat. "I'd give you a final word of advice, but I believe you'll find a way to do the opposite. So for the last time, I'll just say *Carpe somnium*."

Magnus followed his brother toward the tunnels while Patricia herded the sluggish creatures through the door ahead of them. When Mistletoe was alone in the room, listening to their footsteps recede, she sat down and placed the capsule between her teeth. Then she closed her eyes and bit down hard.

14

UNISON 3.0
[beta VERSION]

THE USER KNOWN to his Friends as Adam Trevor stood outside the wrought-iron gate, peering through the bars at the lush apple trees that lined the winding stone path to the door of the magnificent house. Enthralled, he watched as the house sprouted another gabled wing, three stories of immaculate brick with an adjacent tower. All around him, the scattered Profile data of his fellow users flowed in an endless stream through the gate, across the grounds and into the walls of the house. A river of joyful Thoughtstream chatter—disembodied words and floating phrases—joined a flickering mountain of images from a thousand different New Year's parties, all pointy cardboard hats and champagne pellets. Brushing past his arm, a calendar unfolded, sending pages of Event invitations fluttering above the trees to be absorbed into the roof of the house.

Adam Trevor felt a pleasant tug that started behind his eyes and stretched down into his rib cage, as if someone were carefully massaging his insides. He had been away for too long, doing pointless things he could barely remember.

Adam Trevor is finally home!

The front gate swung open, and he started down the path, taking a moment to close his eyes and breathe the hint of ripe apple borne on the gentle breeze. Beneath his feet, stray data filled the cracks between the stones, fleeting impressions of happy times with good Friends. Eventually, after one minute or several days of walking (it was hard to be sure, and anyway it didn't matter), Adam Trevor reached an imposing set of beautiful wooden doors. The archway above was capped by a gargoyle perched like a dog on its haunches, with strangely familiar features and a little clump of sandy human hair. Adam took one last look behind him at the elegantly landscaped grounds and watched transfixed as the serpentine data streams snaked over the gently rolling hills. He put his hand against the door and felt the throb of a billion users' lives. Then he pushed, and the heavy door swung open. He stepped inside.

The tugging behind his face and between his ribs became an unbearable tearing away, like a fist closing around his organs and pulling them out through his skin. He was stunned by the sudden betrayal of the peace and contentment offered by the grounds outside. It was very dark. The pain left his body all at once, like a bandage quickly ripped off a cut. He opened his eyes. It was still dark.

A man's voice said, "Ambrose. I'm going to turn on the lights."

He swallowed. *My name is Ambrose Truax.* He remembered watching Greymatter expand. Someone else had been with him.

"Mistletoe?"

"Afraid not."

The lights came up gently, a dozen embedded fixtures on a dimmer switch. He was standing in a cozy office lined with mahogany paneling and recessed shelves made of glass. Tiny spotlights shone up from beneath each shelf, illuminating dozens of old-fashioned picture frames. A tall, succulent office plant sat beside a massive oak desk that had been darkly stained and buffed to a mirrored sheen. A neat pile of paper was stacked in one corner of the desk, next to a mug that held an assortment of pens and a pair of scissors. The mug said DO I LOOK LIKE A MORNING PERSON?

Martin Truax sat behind the desk, looking crisp and energetic in his familiar blue suit. He was holding a piece of paper with two hands, like an old-time newscaster. He flashed a brilliant smile at Ambrose, who flinched as the white teeth seemed to sparkle in the air a second longer than the smile.

"I thought it best to dispense with your mask," Martin said. "The Adam Trevor Profile doesn't suit you. Antique furniture?" He shook his head and set the paper aside. Something vibrated deep within the walls, and Ambrose thought he saw a pale human ear sprout from the plant before becoming a plump green leaf. He focused on his last clear memory: Mistletoe's abrupt disconnection.

"What did you do with her?" Ambrose asked.

"Nothing."

"How about Len? Was that nothing, too?"

"I had him safely immobilized. The disruptor merely stunned him. He's my *son*, Ambrose."

"Unlike me."

"You're the future."

"I saw him die, Dad." Ambrose winced. He hadn't meant to

call Martin *Dad* ever again. And he was angry at his own brain for automatically triggering a sense of professional awe. Even now, part of him felt like he should be presenting some kind of detailed report.

"But you've been seeing other things, too," Martin said.

The plant rustled and presented Ambrose with a bottle of dark, fizzy liquid. The bottle was sweating little beads of water, as if it had just been pulled from a bucket of ice. Martin clasped his hands together and leaned back in his chair. "UniCola?"

"I'm not thirsty. And I know what I saw."

The bottle shrank back into the leaves. The plant drooped. It looked disappointed.

"Do you?" Martin asked. "Think back to the rapid deterioration of the Level Seven test subjects who preceded you. Your mind is no different, Ambrose. It needs regular calibration. Let me give you your life back. Full Process Flow ability, position at UniCorp. Everything."

Martin leaned forward, setting his elbows on the table. The picture frame on the shelf above his head displayed a candid image of a younger Martin Truax sitting on the grass of the Gen-Farm in the New England Expansion. Next to him, Ambrose and Len buried their faces in two enormous ice cream cones. Ambrose remembered the taste: creamy vanilla synth-dairy, right from the source.

"We were a family once," Martin continued. "I know I've been preoccupied lately, but things can go back to the way they were."

"You remember what you got me for my birthday last year?"

Martin's face was a rigid mask.

"New Process Flow assignments. You doubled my work-load." Ambrose's heart was pounding. A few days ago, he never would have said these things. A few days ago, he didn't even know he felt this way. His eyes went to the image on the shelf. "It would've been nice just to get some ice cream."

"Sometimes I wish I could take it all back," Martin said softly, "and keep you away from UniCorp. But there were moments in the course of our workday when I'd be struck by some little familiar gesture you would make with your arm, and I'd be aware that I'd transferred some deep part of me to you. I'd feel like the luckiest father in the world, working side by side with my son."

The picture on the shelf changed to an older scene: white sand dunes on the beach at the UniCorp Hawaiian Retreat. Martin held baby Ambrose, while Len toddled along, ankle-deep in the sparkling blue green water.

"Help me build the future of this company," Martin said. "Come back home."

"First look me in the eyes," Ambrose said, "and tell me right now that you didn't put me together from some instruction manual."

Martin met Ambrose's steady gaze. The whites of his eyes shone brighter than his teeth, blinding and terrible. Ambrose put his hand in front of his own eyes to shield them from the glare. The office plant rustled. The walls expelled an absorbed Thoughtstream like a gust of hurricane wind that sent him to his knees. A stray update passed through his mind.

Kelly Peterson is superpsyched to be getting a puppy today!

Ambrose shook it off and returned to his feet. The top of Martin's head was a wavy strip of mahogany paneling connected by a thin strand to the wall behind him. His eyes were hollow black pits. His nose and mouth fused into a scaly, elongated snout.

The snout grinned. Rows of white teeth gleamed.

Ambrose heard the door slam behind him and turned. Mistletoe stepped into the office.

She had come back for him.

"Ambrose," she said, joining him in front of the desk, studying his face. "Are you *you*?"

"I'm me."

"And I'm his father," Martin said. Ambrose turned to find Martin looking fully human again, slouched a little in his chair with his legs crossed at the knee. "Nice to meet you, Anna. I hope your journey here was nice. I did everything I could to make the place easy to find."

Mistletoe glanced around, taking in the shelves, the plant, the picture frames. Then she studied Martin's face while he tapped a fingernail on the desk. Ambrose counted six taps before Mistletoe spoke.

"We've met," she said. Then she told Ambrose, "I had a dream we were tiny babies. There were more like us, but they didn't work right or something, so he threw them in a big tub. They were all dead and just . . . floating. We were the only ones who made it."

She turned back to Martin, and her blue pigtail brushed Ambrose's face. He realized he would have come back for her, too.

"Innovation requires sacrifice," Martin said. He reached behind his chair and pulled open a door that had been hidden within the paneling.

A dense web of glittering status updates—gossamer trails of **YAY! BetterTacos for dinner!** and **Anybody know a good tongue modification service??**—interlaced with raw Profile data. Some user's holiday pictures burst from the web and splattered across the doorway. Before they were sucked back inside, Ambrose saw a big black dog with a fuzzy Santa hat and a massive pile of red and green gifts. These were replaced by someone else's Friend list, thousands of tiny faces that dilated and stretched to slurp hungrily at the raw data as it flitted and spun away.

Hypnotized by the chaotic beauty, Ambrose watched until a pattern emerged. Thoughtstreams braided and thickened like DNA strands, working in time with other strands to create a pistonlike motion within the web. It resembled the inner workings of an ancient combustion machine, nourished and powered by Profile data.

Ambrose shivered. The thing—the *engine*—radiated an inhuman chill that corrupted the bitmapping of the office. Little fleshy patches of Martin's face appeared within the leaves of the plant. One leaf was composed entirely of nostrils. Ambrose tore his gaze from the doorway to look at Mistletoe. He could see through her neck to the wall on the other side. Her pigtail slithered through the empty space.

He blinked, and she was whole again.

"Twitterbrained doorway," she said.

"It's some kind of engine," he guessed. "Taking fuel from all those user Accounts."

"Allow me to present the heart of Unison 3.0," Martin said, standing up. A thin tendril of negative space from the center of the doorway licked the edge of his face, stretching his mouth into a frozen skeleton smile three feet long. Then it snapped back into place. "The gateway to ourselves. I'm pleased to give you the opportunity to beta test its capabilities."

"Beta test?" Mistletoe asked.

"It means we're lab rats," Ambrose answered. And to Martin he said, "I'm done with this."

Martin shrugged. "You're free to go. Just remember, without calibration, your mind will fragment completely in a matter of days. What's the point of going irreversibly insane when the antidote is within your grasp? I don't want to lose you."

The plant began to leak a yellowish, foul-smelling fluid onto the floor. Ambrose wondered what it would feel like to lose control of his mind forever. Would it hurt? Would he be able to remember what it felt like to be normal?

"All you have to do is make a single new Friend," Martin said, "and you can have your life back."

Mistletoe grabbed Ambrose by the sleeve. He noticed for the first time that he was wearing a dark blue suit identical to Martin's, right down to the gold *U* on the lapel.

"Let's *go*, Ambrose."

"And Anna," Martin continued, undaunted, "the same goes for you. A single new Friend, and your aunt Dita is free to live her life in peace."

Mistletoe froze, still gripping Ambrose's sleeve.

Martin reached down behind the plant and produced the end of a long yellow scarf, which he wound around his hand twice before trapping it in a fist. He pulled up and dragged a middle-aged woman to her feet. The scarf was wrapped around her neck so that it became a short, choking leash. Her breath rasped in and out as she clawed at her throat.

Mistletoe dropped Ambrose's sleeve and ran to her. Martin yanked the leash and the woman stumbled backward.

Mistletoe stood helplessly. "Aunt Dita," she said softly.

Dita tried to speak. Her words were feeble croaks. Her eyes filled with tears. Mistletoe cried out, "Stop!"

"All you have to do is walk through the door," Martin said. "You'll meet a new Friend and accept her Friend request. And then your aunt Dita is free."

Mistletoe didn't say anything. Ambrose could feel himself losing her. The puddle beneath the plant gave off a sharp vinegar stench. In the doorway, Thoughtstreams intertwined like nonsense haiku.

Grand Opening Sale
Love always and forever
Subcanopy trash

Ambrose wondered if Martin was bluffing. This was the epicenter of Greymatter, deep within the operational core of Unison, and Martin had the primary Admin Deck. Dita's presence here would be easy to fake.

"It's a trick," Ambrose said. "That's not really your aunt Dita."

Mistletoe was standing in front of the door, shivering in the freezing blast of the swirling engine. She looked over her shoulder at Ambrose. He had never seen her so helpless, and he didn't need his Process Flow ability to tell him what she was going to do.

"I assure you, it's she," Martin said. "My men apprehended her before she was able to detonate herself along with her house." He tugged on the end of the scarf. Dita's eyes went wide in terror.

"Mistletoe," Ambrose said, "stop listening to this. Look at me."

Martin pulled the scarf until Dita was inches from his face. Then he leaned in and gave her a kiss on the cheek. "I suggest you get going, Anna. Your new Friend is waiting."

Ambrose moved to hold her back. The office plant, suddenly a nest of human fingers, pinched his skin while a vine wrapped around his leg. He could only watch as Mistletoe's shoulders heaved with her sobs. The doorway seemed to ripple hungrily in anticipation.

"It's okay," he said. "I'll find you."

Mistletoe gave him a tiny smile before disappearing through the door. Her pigtail hung like a frizzy blue comma. Then it was gone.

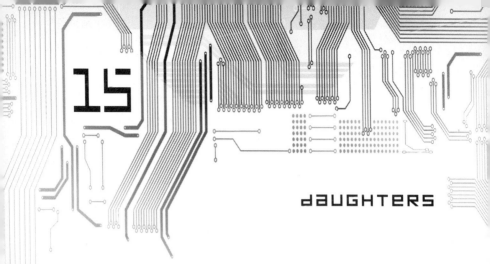

15

MISTLETOE bECaME the eyes of Unison. An old woman embraced an old man, and two wet spots appeared on his shirt where her tears had been absorbed. A little boy urged his brand-new scoot down a grassy slope in a topside park. Throngs of happy revelers in ESCU holo-shirts clinked glasses.

Mistletoe became the ears of Unison. Microblogged thoughts and conversational fragments gathered like loose change in her mind. She learned billions of inconsequential facts like **Sick day!** and **Running late thanks to ESC's perfect traffic control system.**

Mistletoe became the soul of Unison. She burned with envy at more talented people. She studied hard to fulfill her dreams. She failed. She succeeded. She always wanted more. She hated her parents, homework, her boss, her kids, her neighbors, herself. She loved all those things, too.

She cried.

LOL!

She tried to scream and discovered that Unison had taken her voice. Her thoughts were moving in slow motion, as if her brain were underwater. She flailed and thrashed through the thick, chattering air that surrounded her. Eventually she worked her way back to the doorway. The office was just on the other side. She stepped out into normal, breathable air. Her head unclouded. The first thing she noticed was the smell, a pleasant hint of smoky wood and lacquer. The vinegar stench from the leaking plant was gone. It was as if Unison had just decided *this* was the smell of a fancy office.

She blinked away the residue of raw data and looked around. Aunt Dita was gone, too. It struck her that Ambrose may have been right. Martin Truax was the brains of Unison, and it wouldn't have been hard for him to make a vision of Dita appear in the office.

"Ambrose, let's—"

Standing where Ambrose had been was a girl who looked like Mistletoe. *Invisible mirror*, she thought. *Another trick.* Martin was sitting at his desk, watching her expectantly.

"Welcome," he said. There was something not quite right about him, as if in her quick absence he'd managed to get a tan and gain some weight about his face and neck. He'd also darkened the sandy waves in his hair to a solid, younger-looking brown. And his blue suit had brightened to an ugly shade of aquamarine. The mug on his desk said EXECUTIVE OF THE YEAR.

Even more perplexing was Mistletoe's reflection. She was wearing a sleek topside outfit, a ladies' business suit with crisp, pleated black pants and a steely gray blouse. And there was something else . . .

"Hi!" said her reflection, extending her hand. "I'm Anna. I'm really looking forward to being your Friend."

No pigtail—that was it. This Anna had neat, close-cropped hair that looked as if it had never been scented or dyed. Her brightly severe expression gave a distinctly grown-up, corporate impression. Mistletoe felt like she was the target of a complicated practical joke.

"Where's Aunt Dita?" she demanded. "Where's Ambrose?"

Anna's smile faltered. "Surely you're familiar with the sequence of events. Haven't you been briefed on the operational flow of the Version 3.0 beta test?"

"I'm supposed to Friend you and then Aunt Dita goes free."

Anna dropped her hand and looked at Tan Martin. She mouthed the words *Aunt Dita?*

Tan Martin shrugged and glanced back and forth between the two of them before finally saying to Mistletoe, "I apologize for any confusion my counterpart has created on your end. Now, please commence your Friendship."

"If you don't tell me what you've done with them, I swear I'm outta here."

Tan Martin looked at her quizzically. "You've practically fulfilled your purpose. Why come all this way if you're not going to Friend yourself?"

"I don't even like myself that much."

Anna said, "You *do* know who we are—I mean, you and I— right?"

Mistletoe ignored the girl and studied the office. The shelves were cherrywood rather than glass. And instead of framed images, they held wiry metal sculptures of birds.

"What is this place?"

Every part of Mistletoe screamed *GET OUT.* The sudden pileup of things she didn't understand was making her light-headed. But she had used her last login capsule. If she shimmered out now, Ambrose might be gone forever.

"We're the same," Anna said. Her eager smile made Mistletoe want to slap her. "On the genetic level, there's an equal part of me in you, and you in me. We're counterparts. Genetic equivalents. Hybrid twins." She brightened the smile. "Whatever you like."

"You work for this guy?" Mistletoe asked, poking her thumb at Tan Martin.

"Creator-Director Truax?" Anna said, puzzled. "Of course."

"Then I'm nothing like you."

"Our DNA indicates otherwise."

Mistletoe felt feverish, covered in a slimy layer of sweat. She was in a nightmare. Somehow Ambrose's mind sickness had infected her, and she was hallucinating. Without really thinking about it, she brought her hands up to the sides of her head and held her palms an inch from her temples.

Escape.

"Anna, Friend her now!" Tan Martin yelled, vaulting over the desk. The office plant unfurled a leafy vine toward her ankles. Anna looked frightened and confused.

Mistletoe thought of the yellow scarf choking the life out of Aunt Dita. *It isn't real,* she told herself. *Ambrose is right.* Besides, Tan Martin didn't even know what she was talking about. She had to shimmer out, or she would lose what was left of her mind.

Tan Martin loomed above her, a look of fierce desperation on his chubby, artificially boyish face. He reached for her wrists just as she slapped her palms against her temples, closing the logout circuit.

The room receded to a single distant point.

Her mouth tasted warm and coppery, like a pre-Unison coin.

She opened her eyes. It was dark inside Magnus and Ivor's wire trunk. The floor was much more comfortable than she remembered. She sat for a moment, thankful to be back in the subcanopy reality she understood. Then she coughed up a thick gob of phlegm.

If she ever saw Deirdre O'Hanlon again, she'd be sure to tell her she agreed with Pyotr: they were better off without Unison. The greatest social network in history was simply an endless cycle of confusion and frustration. She had tried to do what Martin had asked of her to save Dita, but then Dita was gone and Martin was different and he had no idea what she was talking about. What was the point of it all?

She decided she would grab Nelson and hit the streets. She would go back to Aunt Dita's bombed-out house and poke around for evidence. Then maybe she could determine if Martin really had kidnapped her or if she was simply gone.

Ambrose would just have to help himself until she could figure out another way to log back in. Maybe Sliv knew someone who could hardcode her palms.

As she stood up, a pleasant white glow illuminated her surroundings. The wire trunk was gone. And the brothers' underground lab had become the living room of a posh topside apartment. Her anger flared, sudden and hot.

"I'm still in friending Unison!" she screamed.

"I recognize the keywords but not the command," the room

replied in a soothing, gender-neutral voice. "Please rephrase or authorize a thought scan to determine your intent."

"Kill yourself," Mistletoe said.

"Going offline," the room said. "Good-bye, Anna. Have a pleasant day."

Mistletoe made a fist and looked around for something to punch. A circular table in the center of the room projected an enormous externalized image of Tan Martin with his arms around the shoulders of Mistletoe's corporate twin and a boy who looked like a taller, more beautiful version of Ambrose, with high, almost feminine cheekbones.

"Wait!" Mistletoe said. "Where am I?"

"Your designated UniCorp living space," the room said. "Apartment 1763X on the ninety-eighth floor of a four-star luxury atmoscraper purchased by Creator-Director Truax and repurposed for upper management."

"So I'm not in Unison?"

"You returned from Unison exactly two minutes and forty-one seconds ago."

One of the living-room walls was a single piece of floor-to-ceiling glass darkened by a smoky tint. Mistletoe pressed her palms against the glass, and the tint dissolved to reveal a dizzyingly panoramic view of Eastern Seaboard City. The apartment looked down on a few neighboring buildings—one of them had a roof made of yellow sand speckled with red and white tents—and the grid of empty streets far below. In the distance, the green square of the ESCU campus interrupted the steady progression of atmoscrapers. Poking up beyond the campus, the curved apex of Shimmerdome Nine sparkled in the afternoon sun. She had never seen the city from such a height, and it took her a moment to realize what was wrong: the streets were almost completely empty. She had spent her entire life staring up through the canopy at the ESC traffic flow and had been certain of one thing: it never ended. But now—or here—there were only a few stray cars dotting the streets below. Where were the overlapping patterns of elevated traffic? She ought to be getting a sense of movement and geometry, of lines feeding lines and splitting off into more lines. But ESC was a ghost town. It was impossible.

She had a queasy thought. "I need a mirror."

The room complied, and the doorway to the kitchen became an opaque sheet of glass. Mistletoe looked exactly like eager, preppy Anna, her topside twin. Her pigtail was gone. She was wearing that awful businesswoman outfit.

"Who am I?"

"Anna 53. UniCorp Associate. Department: classified."

She had shimmered into her twin's fleshbound body. It was true: they shared DNA. She pinched the skin of her forearm, touched her stomach beneath her blouse. It felt like her own.

"What happened to all the cars?"

"Fleshbound commuting in Eastern Seaboard City is illegal without a permit. Ninety-eight percent of human interfacing is accomplished via Unison."

"No. There are millions of cars. I've seen them. I've been in a cab."

"Fleshbound commuting in Eastern Seaboard City is illegal without a permit."

"Right. Thanks." She stepped away from the mirror.

"You seem to be disoriented. Would you like me to play some music designed to stimulate your brain functions?"

She ignored the voice. At the window she looked out across the city. She thought of all the things that had been different since she stepped through the doorway: the office décor, Martin's appearance, the ESC traffic flow. It was as if someone had built a detailed model of the world for a vast museum exhibit but failed to get everything right. In this museum version, Anna 53—*me*, thought Mistletoe—was a willing participant in the Unison upgrade. Which meant that here, Anna had grown up side by side with Ambrose and become a happy UniCorp overachiever. There had been no brazen rescue. She hadn't been stashed away beneath the canopy. She hadn't been kept hidden and lied to. She hadn't messed up so many lives. So what about Jiri and Dita? Were they alive in this place?

"Hey!" she yelled at the room.

"Please select a composer from the following choices: Mozart. Debussy. Bach. Beetho—"

"Show me how to get to Little Saigon."

Her neighborhood was all false perceptions and fleeting glimpses. She wandered in a daze, afraid to touch anything for fear that her hand would pass right through and prove this world's—or her own—lack of substance. Every few minutes, her heart raced and she had to stop walking, close her eyes, and take a deep breath. Her fingertips tingled and lost feeling.

Streets that were supposed to bear left turned sharply to the right, and yet still brought her to the same place. An old-fashioned barbershop was familiar down to the squiggly graffiti on the door, but the person lounging out front was a fat woman rather than the man with the bulbous nose who had owned it since she was a little girl. An apple she stole from a street vendor tasted exactly like an overripe peach. She took one bite and tossed it away.

She stopped when she saw the pudgy little boy dart around the side of a parked flatbed transport stacked with old rubber wheels. A dangling sign advertised CHUCK'S TIRES. She followed the boy into an alley, where he joined three kids throwing eleven-sided holo-dice against the brick wall. She stood out of sight and listened until the little boy sneezed.

"Sh-sh-sham-poooooo!"

She stepped into the middle of their game. Shampoo paused, the holo-dice glowing in his curled hand.

"Hey, what's the notion?"

"I just wanted to apologize for scaring you the last time we ran into each other."

Shampoo squinted up at her. He wasn't quite as dirty as usual, and his eyes were two different colors—one green, one blue. He wiped his nose with the back of the hand that held the dice.

"C'mon!" said one of the other kids. Mistletoe watched Shampoo search her face.

"Um," he said at last, "I think you got the wrong person."

"The other day you saw me in the doorway of Jiri's junk shop. You called my name, but I was trying to hide so I got mad at you."

He shifted nervously from one foot to the other. "I don't remember that."

"It's fine. My mistake." She rummaged in Anna 53's pocket for something to give him and came up with a gold *U* lapel pin. "Want this?"

Shampoo looked at her suspiciously.

"Take it. It's yours."

He reached up and grabbed the pin. "Thanks."

"Wipe your face," she said, and left the kids to their game.

It was true: Mistletoe was a stranger in this place. It was a little sad knowing this mostly familiar subcanopy world existed without her in it. As she picked her way through the crowded street toward Dita's shanty-stack, her thoughts began to drift. Was Anna 53 trying desperately to shimmer back into her body? Mistletoe was glad to be out of signal range. She imagined the two of them jockeying for brain space. Being trapped with that girl would be a living hell. But maybe Tan Martin would just let her go. Maybe he had others. In this world she was Anna 53. Did that mean Anna 1 through Anna 52 were alive somewhere?

At the bottom of a narrow path that wound its way up the stack, Mistletoe passed two little girls tossing a bright green conch shell back and forth. When she turned onto Dita's street, she was so relieved to see the house intact that she almost hugged one of the teardrop shrubs. As she approached the maroon door (it had always been blue), she glanced to where the street dead-ended into the side of the absynthium bar. A poster, its bottom half torn away, said TWO FOR ONE.

She walked up the front step and stood poised to knock, her fist an inch from the door. She wondered what would have happened if she had Friended Anna. What was the next phase of Version 3.0? What, exactly, was she supposed to be beta testing? If she stayed in hiding down here, she may never know her true purpose. She thought about that for a second.

Then she knocked.

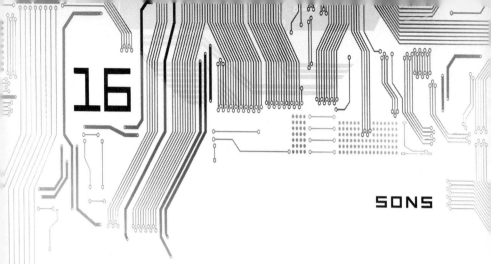

MARTIN GAVE the yellow scarf a vicious tug. Dita vanished. The scarf dangled from his hand, then he tossed it to the brown, decaying plant.

"I'm sorry you had to see that, Ambrose."

"Where is she?"

"The real Dita was vaporized several days ago. She succeeded in blowing herself up when my men surrounded her house. This Dita was just a basic A.I. Profile."

"I mean Mistletoe."

Martin crossed his arms and stared into the doorway at the data storm. He extended a finger and a Thoughtstream whipped into the office to attach itself to the tip. Martin flicked his wrist and the phrase **srsly webbed feet!** dripped from his hand and fell to the floor.

"There is a parallel reality similar to our own," Martin said. His back was almost fully turned. Ambrose held his palms a few inches apart. He couldn't shimmer out until he figured out what had happened to Mistletoe.

"You mean an infinite number of parallel realities," Ambrose said. This was basic grade-school physics.

Martin turned and walked back to his desk. Ambrose put his hands behind his back, holding his wrist.

"But how many of them share an identical social network?" Martin asked. "Just one that I've been able to find. Or, should I say, that found me."

"The original transmission," Ambrose said. "Our design instructions." He wished for his Process Flow ability to fall into place and drag his thoughts toward a logical endpoint. But since that was impossible, he took a guess.

"All this Profile data is strengthening the connection between our worlds. The social networks are the bridge, and this is"—what had Martin called it?—"a gateway to ourselves."

"The next level of Friendship," Martin said. "Now, the most important question is how much to charge users for the unprecedented opportunity—"

Ambrose stepped back as an astonishing figure burst from the doorway.

"—to Friend themselves."

The figure was a boy who could have been Ambrose's taller twin. The bones in his face were different. Kind of girlish, thought Ambrose. And he wore a light brown suit with thick red horizontal stripes.

Ambrose and his twin sized each other up. Then the twin held out his hand. "I'm Ambrose 47. I look forward to commencing our Friendship."

"That's quite the suit you got there."

"The differences between our societies, while relatively

small, will seem alien at first. I suggest that in order to make our Friendship successful, we focus on UniCorp business and keep the jokes and sarcasm to a minimum."

Is this what I sound like? Ambrose thought.

Ambrose 47 thrust out his hand again heartily.

"Please, Ambrose," Martin said, "save your mind. Accept the Friendship, and we'll prep the lab for calibration."

"Then what happens?" Ambrose asked.

His twin looked confused and turned to Martin. "Has he not been given a comprehensive briefing?"

"That's none of your concern," Martin said. The plant was a pile of brown leaves mixed with the viscous puddle on the floor. The picture frame was empty. "The only thing that matters now is your Friendship."

"Ambrose, you and I will seal the bond between our realities on this side of the gateway," Ambrose 47 explained. "The two Annas will do so on the other."

"I love you, Ambrose," Martin said.

"It's an honor to maintain the gateway," Ambrose 47 said. "We'll be contributing to the greatest projected profit margin in UniCorp history."

"Maintain the gateway?" Ambrose looked at Martin, who had come around to the front of his desk. "You built us to become some kind of living portal?"

"User Profile data is volatile," Ambrose 47 said. "We are capable of controlling it."

"That's enough," Martin said, stepping toward them.

"Our DNA has been properly fortified to exist in both worlds," Ambrose 47 said proudly, "and to absorb a truly spectacular amount of energy."

"You're a human being, Ambrose," Martin said. "You're my son."

"If you'd like a moment alone to discuss this, I'd be happy to shimmer out," Ambrose 47 said. "I'll need your fleshbound body, of course, Ambrose."

"Sure," Ambrose said. "It's in stasis alongside Martin's."

Ambrose 47 looked surprised. "At the Gen-Farm?"

Martin backhanded Ambrose 47 across the face.

Ambrose slapped his palms together.

Back in the hole with Len's UniCorp security car, Ambrose kicked the dirt wall. He rode a wild surge of shame and anger. He felt like the most pathetic kind of Tetra Jack loser, one who gets beaten and humiliated by smarter players and keeps coming back for more punishment because, every time, he thinks he finally *gets* it. The Level Seven procedure had been Martin's trump card, and he'd played it so well that Ambrose had practically begged to go under the laser.

He hopped into the car. The ceiling of the subterranean room slid open, revealing a perfect square of slate-colored northern dusk. He nosed up out of the ground and tore across the flatlands at the edge of the forest. In his anger, he pushed the car to full throttle. Pine trees blurred past. The sky was tinged with spectral claws of red and orange. To banish any unwanted visions, he thought of Mistletoe and wondered if she'd actually Friended the other Anna. He couldn't help but picture the Profile data rippling beneath her skin like slimy parasitic worms.

He thought of what he was going to do if he found his father—*Martin,* he screamed at himself, slamming his hand through the glow of the dashboard controls—and hoped he'd have the guts to go through with it.

Then he blanked his mind and focused on the high-speed burn toward the lights of the agricultural district at the edge of the New England Expansion. He darkened the windshield to block the glow of tiered greenhouses cascading down the sides of atmoscrapers. At the perimeter traffic grid, he slid into the street-level flow, tucking in behind a row of bullet-shaped dairy transports. He let the automatic coordination shuffle him a few blocks closer to the center district, then he engaged the lifts and joined the upper-level grid. He cruised past long, grassy balconies dotted with clumps of sleeping cattle and pulled up alongside the old Gen-Farm's roof pasture. He hadn't been here since the day Len made him flick the marble over the edge.

He eased the car over the top of the scuffed plexi barrier and onto the roof. Ambrose was sure Martin had equipped the building with a fully automated security system. With human guards, even trusted UniCorp Associates, there was always a chance someone would give away the location. But the roof was quiet as he set the car down next to the central irrigation chamber. The cows grazing nearby didn't even flinch at his intrusion.

Outside, he jumped down to the spongy ground. The building had over a hundred floors, and Martin's fleshbound body could be anywhere. The first step was gaining access to the interior. Ambrose poked around the irrigation chamber, but it was a seamless metal cylinder. He wondered if he could punch through it with the security car.

Back at his parking spot, two brown-and-white-spotted

cows had moved to graze a few feet from the car. Ambrose wondered idly why these cows were grazing at night. Were they nocturnal creatures? He didn't know much about the behavior of synth-cows. And now he was having second thoughts about ramming the irrigation chamber.

One of the cows stopped grazing and raised her sleepy eyes to study Ambrose.

"Hey, girl," Ambrose said.

The cow opened her mouth. A clump of grass fell out. A bright orange light blinked on inside her throat. By the time the disruptor poked out, Ambrose had hit the soft ground. The first shot burned a jagged hole through the side of the irrigation chamber. Ambrose rose to a crouch. The second shot scorched the grass where his face had been a moment before. He took two loping steps toward the cylinder and launched himself into the hole, scraping his arm against the white-hot edge as he twisted his body into an awkward dive.

He wondered how far he was going to fall, and what it would feel like to land. Then the percussive shock of freezing water numbed the searing pain in his arm. He was completely submerged. A dim light spun at the edge of his vision. He swam for it, deep into the chamber. The light was coming from a round window the size of his head. The window was in the center of a watertight door. There was a latch. He tried it. Stuck. He was getting dizzy. If he swam back up for air, he didn't know if he'd be able to make it down this far again. He'd be trapped, bobbing in the dark water until his body sank from sheer exhaustion.

He gathered his remaining strength.

I am not human. I was built to do impossible things.

He braced his feet against the side of the chamber and pulled on the latch. Something popped in his shoulder. The pain was distant and unimportant. He closed his eyes and strained. The latch gave. He tumbled through the door. Sputtering, half swimming and half scrambling, he rode the torrent of water that rushed out behind him until he could paddle to his feet. The room was empty and cavernous. The water from the chamber continued to flow from the door in a magnificent arcing spray. It filled the room and pooled above his ankles. Ambrose gulped the air and looked around.

A network of pipes on the ceiling seemed designed to divert water from the chamber. He splashed along beneath the pipes, following them as they ran parallel down a narrow hallway. In order to keep a user permanently inserted, the flesh-bound stasis apparatus had to be kept cooled and hydrated. The Gen-Farm was already equipped for massive irrigation. It was the perfect place. Martin had probably bought the entire building.

Ambrose followed the pipes into a room of open scan-tubes arranged in two rows like the bunks of a quarantined hospital ward. Ambrose walked between the rows, checking each tube. They were all empty. The very last one was closed.

Ambrose felt his brain's instinctive resistance to his hallucinations, feeble and short-lived, before he was overcome by creeping dread and the feeling that there was no turning back. He saw his own face reflected dully in the flat silver surface of the tube. Then he slid the top half open to reveal Martin's face, frozen in rictus. The flesh around his mouth had shriveled to a translucent, paper-thin membrane exposing his pink gums and yellow teeth. His eyes were sunken black spots. A rat's nest of wires sprouted from his temples and between the wisps of thinning hair on top of his head.

Ambrose tried in vain to blink this whole place out of existence.

Martin's lower jaw dropped open. The flesh of his cheeks split, extending his smile to his ears.

This isn't real.

"I wanted us to be happy," gurgled Martin's throat. His useless mouth hung without moving.

Ambrose couldn't keep from answering, despite being vaguely aware that he was having a conversation with himself. The sight of Martin's emaciated, atrophied body made him sorry for what he was about to do.

"I *was* happy," Ambrose said honestly. "But the life you gave me was a lie."

Ambrose reached inside the tube. He disturbed a stench, sickly sweet and cloying. He retrieved Martin's brittle arm. The skin was like a thick jelly; if he pushed too hard, it would turn viscous and slippery in his hand. There was a red wire attached to the center of Martin's skeletal palm.

"There's still time." Martin's voice came from somewhere else. Ambrose didn't look for it. "We can start over."

"I am starting over," Ambrose said. "Just not here. Not with you." He pulled up the other arm. The palm was wired in the same way.

The sinewy tendons in Martin's skinny neck bulged and cracked. Brown fluid leaked from the wounds and stank like rotten meat. Ambrose steadied his trembling hands.

I am stronger than a human being.

He dangled Martin's arms outside the tube.

"You don't have security clearance for my Admin Deck," Martin said. "It's far too advanced for you."

"I was designed to absorb infinite Profile data, remember?" Ambrose braced Martin's left wrist and pulled out the red wire. *I can do impossible things.* He plunged the razor-sharp tip into his own palm. The pain was a fiery talon that shot up his arm and gripped his shoulder.

Martin's weeping throat gurgled. "You need calibration. Don't do this. Stay with me."

Ambrose braced Martin's other wrist against the tube with the bottom of his foot and ripped out the second wire.

"I'm canceling the upgrade," Ambrose said. "I'm giving those people back their lives."

"You're not authorized," Martin said. His head thrashed wildly. The lower jaw snapped up and down. "My Admin Deck is encrypted." The yellow teeth clacked and shattered. "You don't have security clearance."

Ambrose closed his eyes. *I'm strong enough to control my mind.*

"Security clearance is for humans."

Ambrose felt Martin's body go limp. The room was quiet again. He opened his eyes and looked at the fragile body of the man who had given him life. Then he pressed the second wire into his palm. Above him, the silver irrigation pipes withdrew to form the distant vaulted ceiling of a steel cathedral. His senses were deadened except for a cruel awareness of his racing heart. Pressure in his chest choked off the last of his oxygen. *A hummingbird,* he thought. *That's what my heart is like.* He could barely remember his own name and managed to say it to himself only once before his mind went completely blank.

*　*　*

In the depths of a watery dream, Ambrose tasted rust. His mouth flooded with saliva. He swallowed the coppery bitterness, desperate for a sensation to replace the memory of his heart's rapid-fire burnout. The flavor was familiar: more like battery acid than rust. A tickle began in the back of his throat and spread to the base of his skull, a maddening itch that made him want to pry open his head for relief.

He had completed the login circuit.

The itchy-throat feeling inflamed his face. He reached up to rub his skin and found that either his hands were missing or his face had ceased to exist. He had a brief and terrible impression of a black pit where his nose and mouth should be.

When the surge of joy hit, Ambrose was once again aware of his entire body. He felt his back arch like a UniPet cat and knew that he had died and been reborn within Martin's hardcoding. The ecstatic shimmer left behind an inner warmth, as if he'd just swallowed a pellet of tea. He was home—and his home had been vastly improved in his absence. He found himself sitting behind Martin's desk in the Greymatter office. The perfectly calibrated chair made him feel relaxed and energetic at the same time. He leaned back and regarded Ambrose 47 in his absurd brown-and-red-striped suit and tried to see his counterpart as anything other than an insignificant collection of brightly colored data.

Ambrose 47 brushed something from his sleeve and spoke in a distant, unpleasant gurgle. "This is highly unprofessional."

Ambrose winced. He longed to shut out his counterpart and explore Martin's—now *his*—Admin Deck. Unison responded to this desire, and the Deck eclipsed his perception so that the office receded to an image on a screen within a screen, a recording of some grainy pre-Unison broadcast. Ambrose 47 shrank to a distant, squawking blur as Ambrose accessed Martin's corporate Feed, a centralized pincushion of Unison analytics blinking like Eastern Seaboard City at night. The interface was the most beautiful thing he had ever seen. He wasn't just logged back into the social network; he *was* the social network. Data sorted itself according to his own capacity to understand it, obeying his unspoken commands as if he were a teacher silencing an unruly class with a single glare. Impressions of potential users who hadn't even begun to create Profiles were etched in his mind as if Unison had reached out into the fleshbound world, tapped them on the shoulder, and requested their signatures. This universe made his old Admin Deck look like a toy.

In the diminished interior of the Greymatter office, the fuzzy smear of Ambrose 47 was becoming increasingly agitated.

". . . and not only that, it's a violation of the Creator-Director's trust!"

The voice was a mosquito whine inside Ambrose's ear. In that netherworld of pointless distractions outside the confines of the Admin Deck, Ambrose 47 droned on and on. The Deck responded to this persistent annoyance by presenting Ambrose with an Account deletion dashboard. Ambrose queried his counterpart's Profile. All around him the Deck quivered in anticipation. Deleting a user from a parallel reality had certainly never been done before. It would be an interesting case study: if deletion resulted in Ambrose 47's death, at least Ambrose would have baseline data for improving safety in future Unison upgrades. His finger hovered over his counterpart's blinking red name. It felt so natural to be in complete control, to have his decision making fully integrated with the Deck. Eliminating Ambrose 47 would be easier than swatting a fly. So why was his finger frozen in place, refusing his command?

The answer seemed to come from an entirely separate mind, one that he dimly recognized as his own. Deep down, he knew that a fatal deletion *shouldn't* be easier than swatting a fly. He forced himself to look into his counterpart's eyes. With great effort, he reminded himself that Ambrose 47 wasn't just the sum total of Profile data and Thoughtstream updates. *Ambrose 47 has ideas and dreams—just like me.* His outstretched finger trembled as he tried to resist the mounting pressure in his sinus cavity. It was his job to delete Ambrose 47 to see what would happen. Unison was his business. Greymatter was his office. The Admin Deck was his home.

"No," Ambrose said out loud. "This is not how I am."

He curled his finger away from Ambrose 47's tiny name and dismissed the Account deletion dashboard. His forehead felt like it was being slowly carved open by a razor. The Deck knew him better than he knew himself. Stopping the pain would be as simple as reopening the dashboard and doing what a decisive corporate leader like Martin Truax would do.

Ambrose took a deep breath. "I am not like him." He closed his eyes and chased away a horrible vision of himself as a decaying husk in an irrigated scan-tube. "I will never be like him." The pain in his forehead faded to a dull ache.

"What are you talking about?" Ambrose 47's voice was suddenly clear and immediate. Ambrose opened his eyes. His perception of the office sharpened and moved to the foreground of his vision. He was surrounded by glass shelves and empty picture frames. Next to the desk, the plant was a wilted pile of dead leaves and brittle stems. Ambrose 47 took on a distinct shape and crossed his arms. "You haven't been listening to me."

"I just realized that I'm not going to kill you," Ambrose said.

Ambrose 47 studied him for a moment, then moved toward the open doorway behind the desk. "When I deliver my report to the Creator-Director, I'll have no choice but to pronounce the initial Version 3.0 beta test a failure."

Ambrose swiveled to stare into the surging web of Profile information and remembered what he had come here to do.

"Wait!" Ambrose said. His counterpart froze alongside the desk. *He's conditioned to obey commands,* Ambrose thought. *He's been doing it all his life.* "It's my fault the test was unsatisfactory. Martin and I had some unresolved quality-assurance issues on our end that should have been dealt with before your arrival."

"Understatement of the millennium," Ambrose 47 said. "Your Creator-Director *slapped* me. I waited patiently for an explanation, and instead he disappeared. I should have returned immediately."

Ambrose stood up and blocked the door. The Profile data felt like a harsh blast of arctic wind against his back.

"I'll go," Ambrose said. "A representative from my end should be the one to give the report."

Ambrose 47 paused to consider this. His cheekbones seemed to protrude obscenely, like nubs aspiring to become horns. "According to my Process Flow, your agenda no longer corresponds with this initiative."

Ambrose split his perception evenly between the office and the Deck. He had to keep his counterpart on this side of the doorway while he deactivated the upgrade.

"What do you do for recreation in your world, Forty-seven?"

"Enhance my managerial skill set."

Ambrose commanded the Deck to expose Martin's private files, the Version 3.0 programming Len had been trying to locate for the past year. The Deck obeyed. It no longer had any influence over his consciousness. He shuddered to think that he had almost let it mold him into another Martin. Three long data pins flared bright white within the Deck's core pincushion: the Version 3.0 design, programming, and implementation files.

"I used to be just like you," Ambrose said.

"We do share source material."

Ambrose tried to extract the files and felt Martin's encryption push against him like a membrane of superheated plasteel that would stretch but never break.

Security clearance is for humans.

He commanded the Deck to grant him access. The encryption protested with a splatter of glitchy sunspots at the edge of his vision. He grimaced as battery acid flowed into his mouth. The encryption dissolved with a stomach-churning jolt.

"What I mean is, the social network used to be my life," Ambrose said.

"I have two million, three hundred forty-seven thousand and sixty-eight Friends," Ambrose 47 announced.

"Really? I have one." Ambrose commanded the Deck to delete the files, and ran a quick seek-and-destroy for any backups. The three pins vanished. "Her name is Mistletoe."

The walls of Greymatter seemed to breathe a deep sigh of relief as the captured Profile data reversed its flow and began to seep from the doorway into the office. Ambrose 47 blinked as a thick strand of red, white, and blue Fourth of July Event invitations whipped past his head. "I knew my Process Flow was correct." He shook his head disapprovingly. "You've gone insane."

"So I hear." Ambrose took a step back. The tips of his fingers went numb. "Listen, how would you like to be the new president and CEO of UniCorp?"

Nervously, Ambrose 47 smoothed the lapels of his suit. "It's always been the primary objective of my ten-year plan. But you can't just—"

"Let's call it your dream."

"What?"

"Say it's been your dream."

"UniCorp protocol forbids me from expressing—"

"Just say it, Forty-seven!"

"It's always been my dream."

"To what?"

"To one day run the company myself."

"Then congratulations on your promotion."

"I'm not qualified to run UniCorp on *your* side."

"You'll be fine. But I suggest finding yourself a new office."

Ambrose backed into the remnants of the Version 3.0 engine, where he was immediately enveloped by Thought-streams that whipped around him like frenzied eels.

Enjoying a completely unreal salad.

So I told him and he got pretty upset.

Have so much fun and tell your cousin I said hi!

Ambrose caught a glimpse of a red and brown sleeve as Ambrose 47 reached through the doorway and was repelled by the swarm of data. His eyes and ears felt huge as the multitude of sights and sounds skimmed along the surface of his body. The upgrade was shutting down. He moved toward a hazy outline of wan light. A smell like burning hair made him hold his breath. He thought about Mistletoe and tried to put himself in her place: what would she do if she found herself in a new world that wasn't so different from the old one? Where would she go? As he emerged from the wreckage of the life that had been laid out for him, Ambrose was pretty sure he knew where to look.

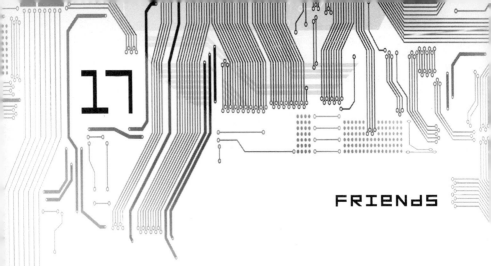

FRIENDS

Mistletoe was wondering if anybody was home when a little rectangle slid open in the center of the door and a hazel eye peered out. She thought it was probably up to her to make introductions, but she couldn't even begin to explain the situation, especially not from the front step.

Then it occurred to her that she didn't have to explain anything, that maybe it was better if she didn't.

"Hi," she said.

The eye narrowed.

"My name is Mistletoe. I'm . . ." What was she? Tired? Scared? Confused? "Thirsty."

The rectangle slid closed. A second later the door swung open.

It was Aunt Dita. Her features were sharper, almost like one of the Chmura Dité, but it was definitely her. She was even wearing the yellow scarf. Mistletoe had to bite the inside of her lip to keep from jumping into her arms.

With a quick look, Dita considered the topside stranger on her front steps. "You're a long way from home," she said flatly, with just a trace of her familiar accent. She didn't step aside or invite Mistletoe in.

"I'm also lost."

Dita laughed. "How'd you manage to get all the way down here?"

"It's complicated." Mistletoe's heart was pounding. *I'm talking to Aunt Dita,* she thought. *And she has no idea who I am.* It didn't seem real.

Dita glanced over her shoulder. "Jiri! Bring water."

Mistletoe heard grumbling from inside the house, followed by loud clattering and muffled curses. Dita flashed a weary smile.

"So . . . do you need help getting home?"

"No," Mistletoe said, almost adding *I am home.*

There was a long pause. Jiri appeared with a glass of cloudy liquid. "Water," he said, handing the glass to Mistletoe without any hesitation, as if thirsty strangers were a way of life around here.

"This is . . . Mistletoe?" Dita said.

Mistletoe nodded, gulping down the water. It tasted sulfurous and a little gritty, and it was the best drink she'd ever had.

"Mistletoe," Jiri said. "Hmpph."

She upended the glass and finished the last drop. She really had been thirsty. They stood without speaking until Jiri cleared his throat with a grating roar and excused himself by holding up his finger. Mistletoe listened to the metallic splat of his spit hitting the kitchen sink.

Dita sighed. "*Maj buhe.* That man's habits."

"I know," Mistletoe said. "And thanks for the water." She was still holding the empty glass. Dita studied her face.

"Do you like tea? We were just about to have some."

* * *

Later, when they were sipping the last grainy dregs of tea from their cups, there was another unexpected knock on the door. Jiri and Dita glanced at each other.

"Eighth New York Quadrant Station around here," Jiri grumbled, getting up from the table.

"This is some kind of record," Dita agreed.

"Wait!" Mistletoe said, leaping to her feet with a suddenness that surprised even her. "I'll get it."

Dita gave her a fierce look. "You expecting someone?"

"I don't know," Mistletoe said. "Sort of."

Before Jiri could step in front of her, Mistletoe raced to the front door. She put her hand on the doorknob and stopped, preparing herself. What if it wasn't him?

Knock, knock, knock.

She opened it.

"Told you I'd find you," Ambrose said. "Nice haircut."

"Nice cheekbones."

"Who's here?" Jiri called from the kitchen.

"An old friend," Mistletoe said, reaching for Ambrose's hand.

acknowledgments

Thanks to my parents, whose boundless love and support should be an inspiration to humans and hybrid creatures everywhere. Special thanks to my brother, whose friendship and conversation I value more than he knows.

I'd be lost without my agent, Elana Roth, whose expert guidance is always delivered with intelligence and wit, and whose Twitter feed is highly entertaining.

Thanks to my brilliant editor, Noa Wheeler, for helping me find the story I really wanted to tell over grilled cheese and fried pickles. Without you, this book would be missing its heart.

Credit goes to Matt Lambert for the usage of *podcast*. Thanks for all your help over the years.

I'm especially grateful to everyone who had the patience and generosity to give detailed, insightful, and honest feedback on a procession of rough drafts and abandoned projects that varied wildly in quality and coherence. Your encouragement kept me going.